WARNING!

You are about to embark on an adventure unlike any you've had before. Reading this book is like taking a wild vacation—you begin each day the same, but you end with a totally new and different story every time you read.

As you go through this book, you'll notice that the action stops just when something exciting is about to happen. You then have to make a choice about what you want to do next. Choose one option and turn to the appropriate page. Continue reading and choosing, creating your own adventure story right up to the exciting finish.

Read the book over and over, choosing a different ending each time. Try following a new track each day and see how many different adventures you can have with just one book. A thrilling vacation in Tanzania is waiting for you; start reading today!

Rhoberg

EAST AFRICAN ADVENTURES

The
Canoeing
Safari

by T.J. Matthews

illustrations by Judy Rheberg

Wycliffe®

Partners in Bible Translation

Orlando, Florida
1-800-WYCLIFFE
www.wycliffe.org

Visit Wycliffe's Web site at *www.wycliffe.org*

You Choose: East African Adventures
The Canoeing Safari
© 2004 Wycliffe Bible Translators
P.O. Box 628200
Orlando, FL 32862-8200

Cover design by Jorge Bustamante. All rights reserved.

Library of Congress Cataloging-in-Publication Data

Matthews, T.J. (Tania Jean), 1983–
    The canoeing safari/by T.J. Matthews; illustrations by Judy Rheberg.
    p. cm.—(East African adventures)
    Summary: The reader's decisions control the course of a canoe adventure set in and around Tanzania's Lake Victoria.
    ISBN 0-938978-35-7
    1. Plot-your-own stories. [1. Canoes and canoeing—Fiction. 2. Adventure and adventurers—Fiction. 3. Victoria, Lake—Fiction. 4. Tanzania—Fiction. 5. Plot-your-own stories.] I. Rheberg, Judy, ill. II. Title.
    PZ7.M43445Can 2004
    [Fic]—dc22

                                    2004014769

Printed in the United States of America

To order additional copies of *The Canoeing Safari*, contact
Wycliffe's Media Resource Center, 1-800-992-5433,
media_resource_center@wycliffe.org

Dedicated to Cliff

EAST AFRICAN ADVENTURES

The Hunting Safari

The Canoeing Safari

The Village Safari

ACKNOWLEDGMENTS

I would like to thank Jesus Christ—for saving me by grace, for giving me the opportunity to write and adventures to write about. I would like to thank all the Kahunda missionary kids—Salowitzes, Hamiltons, Luckeys and Milligans, who shared their lives in Kahunda with me.

Mom and Dad, your consistent encouragement is invaluable. Cliff, thank you for being a wonderful brother—you're the reason I can write about siblings who get along and who love each other. To my African friend Hilda—it was your friendship that enabled me to master the language of Kiswahili and that opened the door to East Africa. I look forward to a day in heaven when we can speak to each other freely without any language barriers.

I would like to thank Dorothea Landers, Carol Dowsett, and Pixie Christensen for encouraging me in the early stages of writing. I would like to thank my teachers—Bridget Howard and John and Glenda Leonard—who all worked with me and encouraged me while the books were in progress. I would also like to thank my colleagues Carol Cruzen, Heather Pubols and Judy Rheberg for seeing this project through to its completion.

And finally, *To Him who is able to keep you from falling and to present you before His glorious presence without fault and with great joy—to the only God our Savior be glory, majesty, power and authority, through Jesus Christ our Lord, before all ages, now and forevermore! Amen.* Jude 1:24–25 (NIV)

—T.J. Matthews

PREFACE

Dear Reader,

Once upon a time a family moved from the United States of America to a village in Tanzania called Kahunda. There were two children in this family, a boy and a girl, who spent their early years living out many of the African adventures you are about to read.

As you may have already guessed, I was one of the children in this family. When I eventually left my village home at age 13, I remembered the adventures from my life in Kahunda and from the other missionary kids who lived there at various times. Kahunda is still a part of me, and so I have written the book you are about to read.

–T.J. Matthews

ADVENTURES IN EAST AFRICA

Two of your best friends, Dave and Danielle, moved to Africa about three years ago. You have been emailing them and hearing all about the village where they live in Tanzania where people bathe in Lake Victoria, deal with African wildlife and don't speak English. This summer they have invited you to visit them, and your parents have agreed! As you board the airplane, you look fondly at your familiar surroundings, secretly wondering if you will ever see them again. It's a jungle out there, right? Anything could happen.

After two nine-hour flights with a stop in London in between, your plane lands on a runway in the huge city of Nairobi, Kenya. In the shove of passengers leaving the plane, you spot Dave and Danielle with their parents "Uncle" Darryl and "Aunt" Debbie waiting for you. As you walk to get your luggage through airport hallways packed with people, Danielle, nicknamed Danny, turns to you. "We'll lay over in Nairobi for a couple of days until you get over your jet lag. Then we'll fly out to the village. If you have anything you want to find on the Internet, you'd better do it now 'cause this is your last chance. There are no phone connections in Kahunda where we live."

"Think you'll be ready for it?" Dave asks, with a slightly joking tone. You nod.

A few days later you leave the big city on a small plane with six seats. Before take-off, the pilot makes sure that everyone has a seat belt on and points out the vomit bags. You notice that Uncle Darryl keeps one ready. Dave watches the pilot excitedly all the way through take-off, fascinated by the controls.

In just two hours you arrive in the Mwanza airport, step out of the plane straight onto the tarmac, and carry your luggage from the runway over to the airport's waiting room. In Nairobi, most signs were in English. Here everything is in Kiswahili. Uncle Darryl and Aunt Debbie don't seem to have any trouble making the switch.

As you all sit in the waiting room on comfortable couches drinking bottled sodas, you decide to ask the question that has been on your mind since their family moved to Africa three years ago. "Why did you all move to Africa? I know that you're missionaries, but what exactly do you do?"

Uncle Darryl answers, "We're missionaries with Wycliffe Bible Translators. It's an organization that works with people groups to translate the Bible into languages that don't have it yet. Right now I'm working with five Wazinza translators to translate the book of Genesis into their language."

"Why can't they just use the Kiswahili Bible since that's the national language of Tanzania?" you ask.

Uncle Darryl answers, "Though most of them can speak the national language, the Kiswahili Bible generally doesn't interest them. It's not their *heart* language. But now that Wazinza translators are working to translate the Bible into their language, the Wazinza are very interested."

Aunt Debbie continues, "The Wazinza are a people group scattered west of this area. If you include all the related dialects, the group probably numbers about 250,000 people."

"Hey! The DC-3 is landing!" Dave calls from the door of the waiting room, looking out to the runway. You and Danielle get up to go look.

"Is that the plane we'll be taking to Kahunda?" you ask, surprised. It looks like it could probably hold 20 people.

"No, we'll be taking another six-seater Cessna," Dave informs you. You return your bottles to the refreshment counter and then board your flight to the village.

You fly over the coast of Lake Victoria, looking down at farmland sprinkled with compounds of mud huts situated in groups of three or four. Thirty minutes later the six-seater plane bumps down onto a grassy lakeside strip of land—cleared especially for missionary aircraft—and taxis to a stop. You look at the crowd of people surrounding the plane. Some are smiling; some are frowning. You wonder why they are all staring at you.

"Danny," you say, "these people are looking at me like I'm some kind of space alien; what's up with this?"

"Well, you *are* a space alien to them." She laughs at your puzzled face and explains, "Most of these people have lived in this village and the surrounding ones all their lives. Many have never been to a city. You're a foreigner when you are here. People stare at you just because you're different and a novelty is always worth looking at."

Uncle Darryl puts the luggage in the truck. After a two-minute drive from the airstrip, you arrive at their compression-brick house. "The bricks are made of cement and termite sand," Dave tells you. Lake

Victoria starts about 40 feet from the house and stretches out as far away as you can see.

The house has two roofs: a grass one that is built about two feet over a metal one. "The grass roof keeps the house cool in hot weather and dampens the loud sound of rain beating on metal," Danielle explains. "When it rains on the metal roof at church, you can't hear anything, not even the speaker!"

"Hey, let's go on a canoeing trip to the islands!" Danielle suggests, suddenly changing the subject.

"You see those dark clouds over the water? If we went canoeing, we might get caught in a storm," Dave argues. "I have an extra slingshot. Let's stay here on land and go hunting instead."

"The clouds won't get here until after we come back, and besides, I'm not as concerned about that as I am about the wild dogs in the woods," Danielle says, tossing her hair.

"The wild dogs will leave us alone, but okay, we can go canoeing," Dave concedes. He looks at you and grins. "Well, what are we waiting for?"

(Go to page 6)

"We'll need three paddles. A heavy one for me, a light one for Danny, and one more for you...." Dave pauses. "I guess I'll give you one of the big wooden ones. We'll also need three life jackets and a stool for the person who ends up having to sit in the middle of the canoe."

"We should probably also bring water and a snack in case we get hungry...."

Dave, in a backward baseball cap, is sitting on the family couch, made with two halves of a foam mattress. He's putting on hiking boots.

"Dave, you aren't *intending* to get out on the islands, are you? I was hoping to just paddle around them!" Danielle groans.

"Of course I'm not intending to get out on the islands. That would be dangerous. But all the same...."

"Don't pretend that you haven't been wanting to explore those islands since we got here." Danielle taps her foot.

"That's because those islands are the only unin-habited wilderness in this entire area! Even the church land with its protected trees is crisscrossed by man-made paths. The islands, on the other hand, are truly wild!"

"And populated by *kenges* and huge pigs that I would prefer to observe from the water, not face to face," Danielle cautions.

"A *kenge* is a monitor lizard," Dave tells you. He turns back to Danielle. "I thought you liked animals."

"Smaller ones," Danielle clarifies.

"You know, kids," Uncle Darryl turns around from his computer work and breaks into the conver-sation, "there are other places to go besides the islands. You could paddle along the shorelines. And both of you have been talking about going fishing for some time now."

"If we decide to go fishing, we'll have to get worms first," Dave considers.

"Literally," Danielle laughs.

"What do you mean?" you ask her.

"Well," Danielle begins, "it is generally accepted around here that when one digs in the dirt, one is likely to pick up hookworm or…."

"Shhhhhh! Danny, we don't have to talk about that," says Dave, making a pretence of urgency. A secret grin passes between the brother and sister. You've noticed that grin before, like Dave and

Danielle are trying to hide something from you. "Besides," Dave continues, "we won't be putting our hands in the dirt, well…not much. We'll be digging with shovels."

"Worms are easy to treat," Danielle reassures you. "You just take a couple of pills. Some worm pills are even chewable."

Dave sticks out his tongue in a grimace. "She actually *likes* them!"

You step out the front door. There it is! The family's seventeen-foot aluminum canoe—your passport to adventure. Dave drops a chain with an attached combination lock into the front of the boat and walks off to the storeroom, whistling.

Danielle looks knowingly at you. "The only reason to take a padlock and chain on a canoe trip is to secure the boat while exploring."

"You know, you guys," says Dave, coming back carrying paddles that are sticking out every which way with bright orange life jackets hanging on them, "I've been almost as curious about what is around the left edge of our bay as I have been about exploring the islands. And, of course, fishing would be fun too."

"You would give up exploring for fishing?" Danielle asks in disbelief.

"Just this once," Dave shrugs. "Besides, fishing is fun, relaxing, peaceful. All that *anticipation*.…"

"Well," Danielle says, thinking, "if we follow the shoreline to the right, we'll end up at 'the Point.'" She motions with her arm to a triangular sand peninsula about a quarter of a mile down the beach. "On the other side of the point is the opening to the 'big lake,' or the part of the lake that stretches all the way to Kenya and Uganda. That's the part of the lake the big waves come from. We could paddle just a little ways around the point and go fishing beside the airstrip, but we couldn't explore very far against those waves."

"We should definitely go left," Dave suggests. "We could explore the left-hand shoreline as far as we want to go. We'd have to fight waves part of the way home, but besides *that*, it would be great."

"Or we could go out to the islands like we planned to do originally," Danielle reminds Dave. She turns to you. "This is your trip. What do you want to do?"

(If you would like to go out to the islands, go to page 10.)
(If you would like to go to the left along the shoreline, go to page 17.)
(If you would like to go to the right to fish beyond the point, go to page 22.)

"I'm glad we decided to go to the islands," Danielle says, paddling behind you. "They're the most interesting."

Dave has his baseball cap pulled down to keep the sun, appearing occasionally through the clouds, out of his eyes. The sun glinting off the waves is blinding. He tilts his head far back to see her. "Danny," he says, "why are you so opposed to getting off on the islands? I don't think it would be all that bad."

The old exploring-the-islands-argument has now been officially reopened. Danielle begins outlining the risks. "There could be any number of dangerous things on the islands, besides the various animals we already know of. Those islands aren't your typical movie-type wilderness. You can get an intestine-eating disease if you fall in the water. There are brambles and biting bugs everywhere. There are poisonous plants, loose rocks, snakes...."

"And caves," says Dave dreamily, stroking his paddle through the water.

"You're not listening to me, are you?"

You turn round to see Dave looking at Danielle with a surprised expression. "Were you talking, Danny?"

She heaves an irritated sigh, turns back around on her stool to face the front of the boat and slumps back into paddling.

"Sorry. Yes, I was listening," Dave relents. "I still want to go check out the islands, though. As you said, these islands are not movie-type wildernesses! These are the wild, rugged, real thing!"

Danielle shakes her head. "Switch!" she calls out. You have learned by now that that is the signal to switch paddling arms. When you and Danielle paddled on the same side of the canoe, you inevitably found your paddles colliding. She explained that fishermen sing as they paddle and thus are able to keep in perfect formation without bumping their paddles. You find it more convenient and easier to balance in the small boat if you and Danielle paddle on different sides.

Your arms are beginning to tire from constant work, but you switch paddling sides and arms fairly regularly, and the islands are getting nearer. The first animals that you see are two large fish eagles, circling above your head.

"Those birds have five-foot wingspans, can you believe it?" says Danielle, shielding her eyes from the sun, awestruck. At that moment one of them drops like a bullet and skims its talons over the surface of the water. It comes up empty-handed, however. The fish got away.

You are now paddling around the left side of the first island. Dave and Danielle have told you that there are actually three islands. They are arranged like a large head of Mickey Mouse. The biggest island is probably a mile in diameter. It is a tall mound with thickly wooded and rocky banks and about half as tall as it is wide. You are beginning to understand Dave's longing to explore it.

"*Kenges* at three o'clock!" Danielle whispers loudly, pointing toward the island which is now about 20 feet off to starboard. You watch two big brown lizards, each at least four feet long, scurry over and around the rocks and off into the woods. Now you can identify with Danielle's feelings.

"They always run away," Dave sighs. "Isn't it interesting how those large dangerous lizards are more afraid of us than we are of them?"

"Speak for yourself," says Danielle, with that look that dares him to question how afraid *she* is of monitor lizards. "You know as well as I do that when a monitor lizard is cornered, it can...."

"Danny, we don't have to talk about that." You turn around to see that familiar brother-sister grin. You are beginning to get tired of this.

"You guys, you don't have to be so secretive! You can tell me what a monitor lizard does when it gets cornered. I think I can handle it."

"I was…kidding," Dave says, "but, yeah, you're right. I'm sure we can tell you about *kenge* fighting tactics. The reason that we have been acting secretive is because Danielle and I have heard about some things as missionary kids that we wish we hadn't. We'd probably be better off not knowing about them."

"It's hard, though," Danielle adds. "Our parents don't want us to be *too* sheltered; we need to know enough to stay safe and to face our environment. It's also good to understand that violence, sickness and death are realities, not just special effects on a TV screen. But it is a fact that in a place without policemen, firemen, rescue squads, or modern hospitals, people die more often."

You continue on in silence for a moment.

"Anyway," Dave starts abruptly, "*kenges* defend themselves by swinging their very long, sharp, powerful tails around. You don't want to get hit!"

You paddle into the fifty-foot water channel between the large island and the two smaller ones. The small islands, one about half as big as the other, seem to be adjoining one another over an isthmus of rocks. Out of nowhere, a rumble sounds through the air.

"Was that what I think it was?" Danielle asks fearfully, looking up at the sky.

You follow her line of vision and see a flash of lightning behind the large island. Dave was watching too.

"Well," Dave grins, "if you were thinking 'thunder.'"

"Lightning." Danielle looks scared. Then she continues in a practical tone, "We're in an aluminum canoe. We need to get out of the water."

"My dear sister," says Dave, nodding his head vigorously in approval, "you're *absolutely* right! Which island should we land on?"

"Dave, I didn't mean get off on the islands! I meant try to make it home before the storm gets bad. These islands aren't safe. Besides, the wind is picking up." Already you can see larger waves beginning to flow into the other end of the channel between the large island and two smaller ones.

"It isn't safe to be paddling back home in this electrical conductor either," Dave says impatiently. "Think about it, Danny!"

Danielle flushes and then looks at the islands uncertainly as a louder rumble fills the air. She takes a deep breath. "I still don't like the idea of getting off on an island, but maybe you're right."

"Say no more!" Dave looks like he's going to cheer. "Well, there's no time to waste. So, which island should we get off on?" He gets your attention and begins his tour-guide explanation, "As you are our guest, I feel that the decision of where we get off falls to you." He faces Danielle. "Right, Danny?"

"Just hurry!" She folds her arms and wrinkles her brows.

Dave continues in his lighthearted tone of voice. "Isibinia (that's the big island) is the one with the pigs, goats and caves. Caves, I might add, to shelter us from the storm."

"Small caves," Danielle clarifies.

"Well, yeah," Dave agrees, "but big enough. The next island after Isibinia that I would recommend is Isibinia Ndogo. *Ndogo* means small. It has lizards on it, but not much else, and Isibinia Ndogo Sana (the very small one) isn't even an option. It's so miniscule that we would stick out like lightning rods."

"Dave!" Danielle says. "If we're so eager to get out of the water, why are we sitting around? We need to get moving!"

"So which will it be?" Dave says to you. "Please choose Isibinia, and please choose quickly. I detect a hint of nervousness in our fellow passenger."

Danielle explodes. She looks ready to paddle the boat by herself. "Isibinia Ndogo would be safer; it has fewer wild animals. We also happen to be drifting closer to it. Let's go!"

(If you would like to go to Isibinia, go to page 43.)
(If you would like to go to Isibinia Ndogo, go to page 45.)

"This can't be too bad," Dave reasons, as the three of you drag the canoe down the gray sandbank from their house. "We'll see a lot more people and fewer animals, but there should be rocks to climb, fishing nets to get caught in; I mean, who knows what we'll find?"

"I have an important reminder," says Danielle. "Dave, listen up!"

"What?" Dave stops fiddling with his life jacket clamp and looks at her.

"We have to avoid the men's bathing area at all costs. Look," Danielle says, pointing. You look. The shore curves around for a mile and then juts out at a point far off in the water. Right in the middle of this stretch of shore you see several naked dark-skinned figures standing around on rocks a short distance from the shore. A few are on the beach, putting on brightly colored clothes. It's too far away for you to distinguish any features, but you still wish you hadn't looked.

"We're going to paddle around that point to get to the part of the bay we've never been to, right?"

Dave nods and Danielle continues, "If we head straight for that point instead of paddling around by the beach, we'll cut time out of our trip."

"Sounds good," says Dave. "We've *got* to remember not to paddle too far, since we'll be paddling against the waves on the way back."

Danielle shrugs. "At least we'll be able to go on shore and rest for a while before we try to paddle back."

By now all three of you have your life jackets on. Dave climbs into the back of the aluminum canoe and sits down on the built-in seat. Danielle takes the stool in the middle. You put one foot into the canoe and use the other to push the nose of the boat away from the beach and then climb in the rest of the way.

The three of you back-paddle through the reeds. They screech along the sides of the aluminum canoe like fingernails on a blackboard. Dave turns the boat toward the far-off point, and you're on your way. The waves rolling under the boat give you an added push, so you move along at a fair pace.

"Okay, you guys, don't look to the left," Dave warns. You are immediately tempted to look, but you know what to expect. "There's a naked man standing on a rock a way out from the men's bathing area. A 'statue in the harbor,' you might say. This is great art! What form, what…."

"Dave, shut up," Danielle's voice comes from behind you.

"I wasn't really looking!" says Dave defensively from even farther back.

The three of you paddle on until all of you are sure that you have passed the bathing area. Then you begin to observe the fishing villages on the shore.

"There's the market entrance," Danielle tells you. You see a small section of beach with many wooden boats docked and a wide path leading up a hill.

Dave's job as the lead paddler is to keep the canoe on the right course. You and Danielle serve as the boat's propulsion. You switch paddling sides when you get tired. Pulling your own weight in a canoe is important.

As you near the far shore of the bay, you see a strange sight. A man in rags with a shaggy beard is jumping up and down on the shore and pointing at you.

"What's he doing?" you hear Danielle asking.

"He's nuts," Dave replies. "Actually, I have no idea."

"He's obviously pointing at us, so it's probably just the usual excitement of seeing white people," Danielle decides. The man certainly looks excited.

"Okay, Danny, you're the language expert; what is he saying?"

"I don't know." Danielle frowns. "He's not speaking Kiswahili. No, wait. That was a Kiswahili word! Jesus…is at…Misome…what? This is really confusing!"

"Misome?" you ask.

"Misome is that huge inhabited island behind us." You look back and see it on the horizon. The closer you get to the man, the more frightening he looks. There is obviously something wrong with him.

"Danny, do you think he's drunk, crazy, or demon-possessed?" Dave asks.

"I don't know," says Danielle, "but I don't like this at all. I don't think he's drunk. Those men are usually a bit more subdued. Maybe he's been smoking *bangi*."

"*Bangi?*" you ask.

"*Hashish*," Danielle clarifies for you.

"No," Dave disagrees. "Those men are even *more* subdued."

Dave steers the boat away from the shore as you round the edge of the bay, but the man follows you along the shoreline, sometimes tripping over rocks as he runs but still yelling hysterically. "Dave," Danielle says shakily, "why don't we pray? This guy is starting to scare me. He's saying some really weird stuff, and I just don't know…."

Dave bows his head. "Lord, You know what's going on here better than we do. We know that You have the power to protect us. Please keep us safe from this man, and please make him go somewhere else! In Jesus' name, Amen."

Danielle looks up. "He's still there." The man has begun to do flips, still continuing to scream, but you can feel a definite peace surrounding the boat. "Should we keep going?" Danielle asks.

"We could," Dave responds. "Or we could paddle out into the lake, and come back after he leaves." You look out into the water and see a large island many miles away, blocking all but a short strip of the horizon. You could paddle for hours out there.

Dave turns back around to you. "We want you to have a good time. Would you rather paddle out into boring water, or paddle along the shore with a weird man yelling at you?"

(If you would like to circle out into the lake to try to lose him, go to page 32.)
(If you would like to just keep going in the hopes that he will get tired of following you, go to page 37.)

"I'm glad we didn't try to go to the islands," Dave comments. "The wind is really picking up." You, Dave and Danielle are all down by the shore of the lake, where you have been digging for worms in the wet sandy shore. All of you are careful not to touch the lake water. Dave and Danielle have warned you about bilharzia, a disease you get from a parasite that lives in the water. It eats your intestines if left in your body long enough. There is a treatment for it: biltraside, a nasty drug that kills the parasite. However, Dave and Danielle's family have decided to take the route of never touching the lake water rather than the route of risking infection and treatment.

"Don't the African people get bilharzia too?" you ask.

"Yes," Danielle says sadly, "some of them go in and out of the water all the time. Many become very sick and even die."

"I can understand, though," Dave tells you, "it's really hard to live so close to a lake and not be allowed to touch it—especially on hot days." Bilharzia is contracted simply from putting a warm-blooded body in direct contact with the lake water. The flukes of the bilharzia disease sense the presence of a warm-blooded animal and swarm to it.

"I found one!" You look up to see Danielle squatting in front of the hole she has dug in the sand. A large brown worm is wriggling in it. Danielle grabs the tail, but the slimy worm slips through her fingers and burrows down into the sand. She shudders and sits back.

"Well, get after it!" Dave, who hasn't found any worms yet, is growing impatient.

Danielle digs around. "It's gone." You dig another shovelful of sand out of your hole and notice a thick worm. Dave sees it too and scoops it out of your shovel along with a handful of dirt. He drops it into a margarine container and clamps the lid over it.

The wind off the lake whips through your hair as you continue to dig. Danielle pulls the lid off the container to drop a short worm into it. One especially large worm begins to crawl over the edge of the container as Danielle tries to jam the lid back. She squishes the neck of the escaping worm in the process. With a shudder, Danielle falls back, still clutching the lid. Dave pushes the wounded worm back with one finger, puts the lid on and looks up at Danielle. She is sitting, facing the wind with her elbows resting on her knees and her head in her arms. She looks up.

Dave chuckles, "Danny, you don't have to help get the bait. I know you're brave; I also know that you hate worms. You're free to do something else. We'll share the worms we catch with you."

"I don't hate worms!" Danielle puts her head in her arms. "I just hate hurting worms, or any living creature for that matter."

"Danny," you ask, "if you hate hurting animals, why are you going fishing?"

"Fishing is part of survival and finding food and all of that. I approve of the practice of fishing; I just don't believe that animals should be put through any more pain than is absolutely necessary."

Dave shakes his head with a grin and goes back to digging in the sand. "That's my sister," he says to you. "You'll get to know her eventually. For someone who hates to hurt animals, she's a pretty good fisherman."

"Fisher*woman*," Danielle says from behind him, throwing a handful of gray sand into the air.

"Six, seven…." Dave is busy counting the squirmy worms in the margarine container. "Nine; that's plenty. Let's drag the boat down."

The three of you carry your shovels up the slippery sandy slope and reenter the yard. Simba, their dog, comes trotting out, wagging her tail. Dave drops

his shovel in the storeroom and tousles the hound's
floppy ears. "Yes, we're leaving you. No, you can't
come." You all put on life jackets and then drag the
canoe, loaded with gear and supplies, down the steep
sandy embankment from their house, with Simba
bounding excitedly around you. Dave pushes the boat
out into the water and gets in first. He makes his way
to the back of the boat and sits down. Danielle gets in
next and totters her way to the carefully placed stool
in the center. You put one foot into the front of the
boat, and push off with your other foot. Simba

splashes right into the water, oblivious to diseases that may be in it. The boat slides smoothly away from the shore and then begins to rock in the dark, wavy water.

(If you know how to paddle, go to page 27.)
(If you have never learned how to paddle a canoe through rough water, go to page 30.)

You are paddling toward "the Point." Fishermen pulling nets in from a sandbar shout to you as you go by, but you can't understand what they're saying. Dave waves; Danielle doesn't respond. She explains to you later that in the African culture, it is appropriate for a respectable young lady to pretend she doesn't hear strange men who call out to her. You round the final point, and suddenly the front of the boat is hit with the first of many large gray waves that send cold spray all over you. You begin to paddle hard, yet you know you could walk faster than the boat is going. But the purpose of this activity is to get the *boat* to a fishing spot, so you press on.

"The women's bathing area is just around that clump of reeds, so I think we should stop here!" Dave calls out, pulling into the shore.

"How come you know where the women's bathing area is?" Danielle asks, looking at him mischievously.

"Everybody knows that," says Dave, offended. "How else would we all know which areas to avoid?"

"Actually," corrects Danielle, "I think the women's bathing area is at least two clumps down."

"Well, whether it's 2 clumps away or 20, I still think this spot is fine for fishing," says Dave, exasperated.

"It is," Danielle agrees.

Dave drops the anchor into the waves that rock the boat to-and-fro. You're surprised that they fish so close to the beach. "Now we come to Danielle's favorite part!" says Dave reaching for the margarine container.

"Dave, stop it!" says Danielle, looking frustrated and upset. She doesn't like to be teased about this particular subject.

"Okay, okay. So, Danny, would you like me to bait your hook for you?"

"Always," says Danielle, passing the empty hook at the end of her line back to him without looking. Dave fishes a squirming worm out of the container, pulls it into three pieces, and feeds Danielle's hook through the inside of one of them from tip to tip until the hook is completely covered. He hands Danielle's line back to her and then grabs a fishing pole for you. You stand and reach for the pole with both hands. Dave hands you the pole and, at the same time, one of the other two pieces of worm. As you stand there looking at it, it writhes in your palm and squirts some brown fluid into your hand.

(If this would bother you, go to page 105.)
(If holding a moving part of a worm wouldn't make you lose your cool, go to page 116.)

Dave turns the nose of the canoe into the waves and begins paddling. Danielle is also paddling diligently, but somehow the boat isn't making much headway. You paddle furiously and send a spray of cold water over Danielle. She sputters and then, to your relief, laughs.

"Let me just give you a couple of quick paddling tips," Dave says from the back of the boat. "Paddle on the opposite side of the boat from Danny. If either of you get tired, you can switch sides. Right now you are paddling on the starboard side of the boat, so put your left hand over the end of the paddle and your right hand far down on the shaft. The farther down the better, just not so far that you put your hand in the water. Turn the blade so that it is perpendicular to the side of the boat."

"And then push the water," Danielle adds. "The more resistance you feel, the more you are moving the boat. Also," she adds, "be careful when you are exerting so much force on the water not to let your paddle come flying out of the water, spooning it all over *me*." From then on the boat moves more quickly against the waves.

(Go to page 27.)

"Good decision." Dave steers the canoe away from shore.

As you paddle away, you look backwards periodically to see if the man is still there. Eventually he looks just like a bouncing brown dot. Then all at once you look back and he's gone. "All clear," you say to Dave and Danielle. Dave turns the boat around and Danielle sighs with relief.

"You know, you guys," Dave says, looking concerned, "ever since we began paddling away from shore, we've been drifting. I've been trying to fight it, but the waves around the point are coming from a direction that is pushing us out into the lake and away from home. I'm getting tired."

"Why don't we sit a minute?" Danielle suggests. "We'll rest and then we can try to paddle back to shore. You'll get to use your other steering arm, and if we drift farther away from home, we'll just follow the shore back."

"Easier said than done." Dave grimaces, flexing his sore left arm.

"Why don't we just sit for a minute and listen to the silence? You don't hear quiet like this very often, unless you are deep in a cave."

"Or deaf." Dave's arm appears to be improving. You all sit back and listen. You can hear the waves lapping against the side of the boat and a few bird cries. The atmosphere is utterly peaceful. Dave still looks worried. "You guys, I don't like this. The waves are against us, and I think they're getting bigger. If we want to get home, we need to begin paddling now. Let's head for the shore." He begins to turn the boat back toward the land. All of you begin to paddle hard. Suddenly a rumble fills the air.

Danielle looks at you and then back at Dave. "Thunder," you confirm. Danielle turns white.

Dave speaks from the back of the boat. "I hate to sound dramatic, but that is the signal to paddle for your life. Let's go!" You all begin to paddle hard. The waves are bombarding the front of the boat diagonally from the left, pushing you in exactly the opposite direction from the way you want to go. They are already about a foot and a half high.

"Shouldn't we pray?" shouts Danielle over the noise of slamming waves.

"Yeah," Dave shouts.

"Dear God," Danielle shouts, panicked, "we're out in an aluminum canoe in a lightning storm after being cursed by a strange man. I guess that You already know that," she says more thoughtfully and then continues, "Lord, please help us get to shore. And thank You that You are more powerful than curses and nature." A rumble of thunder concludes her prayer.

The storm is building up. The wind is blowing all around you. The sound of a thousand thunders rumbles toward you from the center of the lake. You all continue to paddle. And paddle and paddle. The waves hit the boat and rock it violently. You don't seem to be making any headway. You just hope that you're at least holding your position. "Sorry, you guys," Dave shouts. "This was a stupid idea. I should have known not to paddle the boat this far from shore."

"Excuse me…Dave," Danielle corrects him and then ceases paddling in order to talk. "The two of us thought this was a good idea; you didn't drag us out here, so don't blame yourself."

"I made an error in judgment that, as the oldest, I shouldn't have!" Dave shoots back, full of responsibility.

Another rumble of thunder fills the air, and your muscles are aching. "Let's just paddle," you shout back. "We can…work…this out…when we…get there."

"True," Danielle agrees. "Arguing over who is guilty is no reason to get fried; let's paddle."

"Thanks a lot, Danny!" Dave shouts. "I really needed that piece of imagery right now!"

Just paddle, you think to yourself.

"We just need to trust God, I guess. There's nothing else that we can do right now." Danielle pauses her paddling to call back to Dave.

Except paddle.

"You're right, Danny," Dave says, and then the talking stops. This is good, because you were about to explode. You keep paddling hard.

"You guys!" Dave shouts. You and Danielle turn around to look at him, and once again the paddling stops. "We have another option besides trying to fight the waves to shore." The boat has begun to drift sideways. And you all strain to pull it back into the right position. Then you pause while Dave continues, "If we paddle parallel to the waves, we won't have to work so hard! We'll have to paddle a lot farther, but we'll probably get to shore more quickly."

"We might actually get somewhere!" Danielle agrees. You follow the waves with your eyes until they meet the shore.

"Mom and Dad will worry, 'cause it'll take so long, but at least they'll know where to look for us.

They'll just come and get us in the motorboat. It looks like a long way to paddle, but it should be easier than fighting these waves, and we need to get out of the water!" He isn't kidding. You have drifted farther out as you've been talking, and you're still hearing thunder periodically. This new idea is sounding better all the time. "There is a downside to my idea, though," Dave warns loudly over the noise of the storm. "When the boat travels parallel to big waves, it's rocked from side to side and very unstable! If we lose our balance, even for a moment...."

"I think we can do it," Danielle interrupts.

(If you would like to try heading straight for shore, go to page 48.)
(If you decide to try to go parallel to the waves, go to page 67.)

You continue along the shoreline. The man keeps following you, yelling unintelligible words. Dave and Danielle try greeting him, but he simply steps up his tirade when he discovers that he has their attention. You all try to ignore him, but you're getting more annoyed. You glide around the edge of the bay and paddle down a new shoreline. The boulders and trees look very much the same as they did before, but now the lake is rimmed by corn and cassava fields rather than people and fishing villages.

The man disappears without warning; all three of you are glad. The silence, or rather the chirping of birds and the noise of the waves, is a welcome relief after hoarse shouting. You pass some women washing clothes and children. The women laugh and shout to each other as you go by. The children stare, wide-eyed and silent, and the mothers take advantage of the opportunity to get as much washing done as possible.

"Somewhere around here we need to stop and rest before going back," Dave says. "The wind is picking up. Let's stop the next time we see a pile of rocks. Rock climbing would be fun."

"Just be sure we climb on rocks that are surrounded by water," Danielle says with a shiver. "If that man jumps out at us from the bushes, I'd like there to be something between us and him." Following her suggestion, you wedge the boat between a small and a large boulder, rising up out of the waves about 20 feet from the water's edge. You all climb out and sit on the large rock watching the lake birds. At least that is what you are trying to do. Dave keeps looking at the canoe, to make sure it isn't slipping out from the rocks. Danielle keeps glancing at the shore.

You can't help but notice the gathering clouds. You hear a whirring sound in the distance to the left. "What's that?" you ask, startling Dave and Danielle.

"A motorboat!" Danielle looks excited.

You wait. Sure enough, a wooden canoe with a motor, piloted by two African men, comes into view. It is towing two other canoes with men in them. "You know what?" Dave says happily. "We may not have to paddle home against the waves after all. Hey!" Dave starts jumping up and down on top of the rock, waving his arms. The men, who have already noticed the three of you, pull the motored boat to the rock.

"*Tunataka lifti!*" Dave calls.

"*Tunataka lifti!*" one man in the first boat repeats in a put-on high squeaky voice.

"*Ndiyo,*" Dave replies in a low voice, telling the man that he is willing to do business on a mature level. The man nods and begins speaking to Dave in his adult voice, rather than the one reserved for children.

"*Bei gani?*" Danielle asks suspiciously.

"You want to settle the price now?" Dave asks her in English.

"Yes, I do," she responds with complete certainty. "We don't want them to charge us a huge amount of money after they have already towed us home. We should settle it now. *Bei gani?*"

The man laughs at her question and gives Dave a "What's she worried about?" look but doesn't answer.

"*Bei gani?*" Dave asks.

The man sighs and then responds in a quick flood of Kiswahili. Danielle translates quietly for Dave, who got lost after the first five words. "He says that he'll give us this ride in friendship; all he needs is a teensy, weensy little bit of fuel to make up for his trouble. He knows our dad has lots of it. He says the fare is usually 10,000 shillings, but he will tow us for half that, as long as we give him enough fuel to make up the difference, 'cause you see, he's our friend. Dave, we can't do this."

Dave replies to the man, who isn't in quite as friendly a mood anymore. The man names a price plus some fuel. "We can't give him fuel," Danielle says flatly. Dave tells him that. The man raises his hands and gets ready to drive away.

Dave shrugs and sits back down. "Oh, well. It was a good idea."

Then the man comes back, serious as a salesman.

"He wants 10,000 shillings to tow us. No fuel," Danielle translates.

Dave shakes his head. *"Mia tano."*

"Five hundred," Danielle translates for you. "He's overcharging us."

"Elfu moja," says the man.

"He says he wants 1,000 shillings," Danielle explains.

"Sound okay, Danny?" Dave asks. "That would pay for the fuel he'll use to take us home, plus give him a little extra money for his efforts. Besides that, he's already got two other canoes paying him."

"It sounds okay," Danielle agrees. The men tie your boat with ropes to the back of the last canoe and then start off, pulling you in tow. As you enter the familiar bay, the size of the waves increases. You would hate to be paddling back right then. "On second thought," Danielle comments, "1,000 shillings doesn't seem that bad."

You arrive back at the house. Danielle runs in to get the money while you and Dave begin pulling the canoe up the embankment. When the man follows you to the house, you assume he's only making sure he gets his money. Actually, he came to ask Uncle Darryl for some fuel, hinting he had been promised some. Dave and Danielle tell Uncle Darryl that the boatman had promised to tow them home for 1,000 shillings, not for fuel, at which point the man claims 2,000 shillings, because of the rough weather. In the end he gets 1,500 shillings because all of you—Uncle Darryl included—are tired of bargaining. At least you didn't have to paddle all the way home in the strong current. Besides, 1,500 shillings—two American dollars—is a good day's wage in Kahunda, so in the end the man is happy with what he got.

THE END

"So we're off to the big one?" Dave says cheerily. "Good. It's the only one with a sandy beach...."

"Dave, just paddle!" Danielle erupts. She turns and begins furiously jabbing the water with her paddle, propelling the boat toward the large island. Scanning it, you spot the small sandy beach immediately. It is the only one in sight.

As you pull the canoe into the small bay, you notice a reptile-like creature about five feet long swimming around in the shallow water. A monitor lizard, maybe? Suddenly it lunges for the front of the boat! You gasp. It isn't a monitor lizard. It's an enormous snake with fangs bared, and it's coming right at you! You are sitting in the front of the canoe, and you can't see Dave and Danielle behind you. You know you have to act immediately.

(If you sit perfectly still, go to page 52.)
(If you scream, go to page 56.)
(If you hit at the snake with your paddle, go to page 58.)
(If you back-paddle quickly, go to page 60.)

"Isibinia Ndogo it is," says Dave with resignation, picking up his paddle and turning the nose of the canoe around in the wavy water. "Though I have to tell you, Isibinia probably would have been more interesting."

Danielle is delighted to be going somewhere, even if it is to an island.

Unlike Isibinia, the land of Isibinia Ndogo is very low and flat. The "beach" is composed of a pile of white rocks that rise about a foot above the waterline. You pull the boat into a small cove between two large, half-submerged white rocks and climb out, still wearing your life jacket. A narrow beach soon gives way to trees and bushes. A lone path disappears into the island brush. The white-rock beach, rimmed with floating water plants, seems to go all the way around the whole island, or at least as far as you can see. You see an edge of what must be the smaller island off to the left, but tall flower bushes obscure the full view of it.

You take a step and slip on a loose rock. Looking down, you notice what looks like the head, shoulder and arm of a large frog lying in the rocks. "Probably a bird did that," Danielle explains, wrinkling her nose at it. Dave is busy trying to chain the boat to a low-hanging tree branch.

As you walk toward the right, you glimpse something below your foot. It is about a foot long, narrow, and reptilian. Instinctively, you startle and jump away from it, almost falling into the water. Danielle looks over quickly and nods her head. "That would be the other half of the baby *kenge*." Sure enough, what you almost stepped on is the body and tail that goes with the head and arm of what you thought was a frog. The back half of the torn lizard looked like a snake at first glance.

Dave comes walking over. "Ugh! Don't they have ants on this island? That should have been cleaned up weeks ago!"

"Maybe it's recent," says Danielle, with feigned indifference.

"So which way are we going to explore?" Dave asks, jittering with excitement. "The path looks interesting. We can hide our life jackets under that bush over there. I'm getting hot." You all take them off and hide them satisfactorily.

"As long as we're exploring, let's see if we can cross over to Isibinia Ndogo Sana," Danielle suggests.

"These two smaller islands are so close we might be able to go from one to the other. I haven't heard any thunder for a while. I think crossing islands might be fun."

Dave rubs his eyes in exaggerated surprise, and then blinks hard. "Danielle says, 'Exploring might be *fun*'?"

Danielle ignores him. "Getting over to that island would be a challenge. Besides," she adds rather sheepishly, "I like flowers, and there are lots of them over there."

"All right," Dave says, looking at you through watery eyes. "So which would you, as our guest, rather do: explore this island or try to make it to the next one?"

(If you would like to explore Isibinia Ndogo, go to page 75.)
(If you would like to try to cross over to Isibinia Ndogo Sana, go to page 78.)

You keep paddling toward the shore. Maybe if you all pull hard enough and quickly enough, you'll make it. The land looks a little closer. It should be. You check your watch. You have been working steadily for half an hour since your last discussion. You look back at Dave and Danielle who are still paddling hard with gritted teeth.

You and Danielle switch paddling sides for the umpteenth time. You've all been paddling for an hour. The waves are two feet high, and you are finally able to see the outlines of trees on the shore. "You guys!" Dave shouts. "My right arm is killing me." Because of the angle of the waves, Dave has been paddling on the right side of the boat for the last half-hour. "I need a replacement!"

"Arm?" Danielle asks. Dave's shoulders droop in frustration. "Okay, Dave, I know what you mean; I'm coming. I just couldn't resist."

"If I paddle much longer, I *will* need an arm replacement but for now I'll settle for a replacement paddler!" Dave trades places with Danielle. "I can only paddle on the left side now, so you'll have to take the right," he yells up to you. You begin paddling on the right.

Within half an hour, Danielle is exhausted and Dave's arm is still hurting. You take Danielle's place in the back of the boat, and Dave moves to the front with his exhausted arm while Danielle resumes her seat in the middle. You have been paddling on the right side for the last half-hour, so within a few minutes you are completely spent.

All of you look at each other and then collapse wearily in the rocking boat, staring hopelessly at the shore. "We gave it our best shot," says Dave. "Now I guess all we can do is just sit here and hope this isn't our time to die."

"I'm kidding," he adds with a glance at Danielle.

"I haven't heard any thunder for a while," Danielle says hopefully, as she lowers herself wearily onto the bottom of the canoe, stretching her legs and flexing her stiff right arm. "Maybe we won't get a storm after all. By the way, what time is it?"

"Five o'clock," Dave responds. "Mom and Dad will come looking for us in the motorboat by five-thirty or six. They'll be worried."

"So how far do you think we'll drift in the meantime?" Danielle asks. The boat has already begun to drift farther out into the water.

"We never should have gone so far out in the first place!" Dave groans.

All of you are spent. "Shall we play a game?" Danielle asks.

"As long as it doesn't involve any arms," you say.

"No," says Dave. "I personally would prefer to take a nap." He sits down on the floor at the front of the boat and pulls his baseball cap over his eyes. You sit down in the same position, leaning your back against the built-in back seat and close your eyes....

"Hey! Hey! Over here!" Danielle is standing up in the middle of the boat waving her bright orange life jacket. You see the motorboat closing in. The lake has calmed down quite a bit since you fell asleep, and the sunset is just beginning. You are amazed at how far you have drifted!

Uncle Darryl and Aunt Debbie pull up beside the canoe. "Are you all okay?" Aunt Debbie calls out with concern.

"We're all fine," you tell her.

"So, what happened?" Uncle Darryl asks, after getting all of you into the motorboat and hooking up a cable to tow the canoe. It is obvious that he and Aunt Debbie have been worried.

"It's a long story, Dad." Dave stretches sleepily and then grimaces as his aching arms complain.

"I'm glad to be going home," Danielle yawns.

You are glad to be going home too, even if it isn't your real home. If missionary life has taught you one thing, it is that "home" is often relative to wherever you are.

THE END

Sitting very still, you watch the snake approach. It slides its head over the side of the boat and goes for your leg! It's time to bail out—you drop your paddle and, in one swift movement, force yourself out of your sitting position and over the side of the canoe. The boat dips under the force of your spring but pops up as soon as you are airborne. Your foot catches on the rim and flips the boat over. Kids and snake fall thrashing into the water. As you drag yourself to your feet in the shallows, Danielle screams nearby.

"What?" Dave yells, staggering out of the water.

"I don't know; something bit me." Danielle is looking around frantically. Then she really screams as she sees the huge form of the snake slide quietly away from her. Dave looks thunderstruck and Danielle looks absolutely terrified. You and Dave drag the upside-down boat onto the beach, flip it over and push it back into the water.

"Danny, get back into the boat." Dave takes command. Quietly she obeys. You and Dave, both sopping wet, climb in after her. Danielle moans, though whether from fear or pain you cannot tell.

"Come on, Danny." Dave puts his paddle aside and leans over. "Let me see the bite. I want to check for poison marks."

"I already checked, Dave." Danielle shows him the back of her calf. "There are two perfect fang punctures right here!" She begins to cry.

"Danny, just sit down in the boat. And don't try to paddle," Dave instructs. "We'll get you home right away." He looks over at you. "Do I have to tell you how important it is that we get home as quickly as possible?"

You shake your head, pick up your paddle and dig into the waves with a fury. You know how urgent this situation is. That was a rattlesnake. You have never seen a swimming rattlesnake before, but you know that it could very well have been poisonous.

The canoe picks up speed as you and Dave paddle with energy and force. You groan as you round the calm side of the island and catch sight of the waters beyond. You will be paddling home against two and a half foot waves! Danielle moans. What choice do you have? Leaning forward, you plunge the paddle into the water and pull back with all your might. The waves violently push you backwards. Dave is praying,

"Oh, Lord, please...." but his voice is lost in the wind. Looking back, you see Dave with the spray lashing his hair around his face. Danielle is lying in the bottom of the boat, obviously alive, but with a more peaceful expression on her face. Occasionally she winces in pain. You see swelling around the bite. Adrenaline pumping, you press on. You never knew that you could do this much strenuous activity. The shore is getting closer, but you're not tired yet. This is incredible! You may never be able to explain it, but you remember Dave's prayer and something about being able to do all things through Christ who gives you strength.

The shoreline is getting closer. You jab and pull with your paddle...again...and again...harder each time, as though you are trying to push the entire lake behind you with each stroke. Suddenly the boat scrapes on the shores of home. You and Dave jump out of the canoe and half-drag, half-carry, Danielle up the sandy hill.

"Mom! Dad!" Dave yells as you approach the house. "Danielle's been bit by a snake!" Aunt Debbie runs to get her medical supplies. She gives Danielle an electric shock on the snakebite. Uncle Darryl tries to radio for a plane. After about half an hour of calling, he manages to make contact with the city. A pilot and plane are available. Two hours after arriving home from the islands, you hear the hum of an airplane.

By then you are all packed. Danielle gets on the plane and promptly falls asleep. The rest of the family seem too anxious to do that.

From the Mwanza airport, you board a second small plane to take Danielle to a hospital in Nairobi, Kenya. Since no one has ever heard of the snake that bit her, no one wants to take any chances. You spend the rest of your time in Africa in the Kenyan city of Nairobi, going to movies and malls and checking on Danielle. You look at all the snake books you can find, only to confirm that no swimming rattlesnake has been documented yet. Your eyewitness report is all you have to go on. In a week Danielle is up and walking around. She doesn't blame you for jumping out of the boat; she theorizes that she probably would have done something similar. Your African visit didn't turn out the way you expected, but Nairobi is an adventure in and of itself.

THE END

Even you are startled by your scream. You look back to see Dave and Danielle frantically trying to peer around either side of you. "It's a snake!" Danielle shrieks and immediately begins to back-paddle.

"Wow!" Dave exclaims. Then, realizing the gravity of the situation, he begins to back-paddle too. The boat slides back out of the bay and into the channel. The snake bares its fangs at you, then dives underwater.

"Dave," Danielle says, shaking. "We need to get out of here. We don't know where that thing is going to resurface."

"Over there!" Dave calls from the back of the boat. He points across the channel to Isibinia Ndogo. Rustling vegetation catches your eye. You catch a glimpse of a snake slithering over a white rock on the shore of Isibinia Ndogo. You breathe a sigh of relief.

"We're not out of the water yet," Danielle reminds you.

"Well, at least now we know that it's not on Isibinia anymore," Dave comments. "Okay, gang, ready to try again?"

Try again? You were just face to face with a potentially poisonous snake, and he wants to go back?

"It's either that or paddle home in a lightning storm," Dave adds. Now that you think about it, it would be possible to get off on the island but not go inland. You could wait out the storm on the beach.

"So," Dave is disconcerted by your silence, "are we going to try again?"

What is your response?

("My feelings exactly. Let's try again!" Go to page 165.)
("I think I would rather wait out the storm on the beach." Go to page 182.)

The snake backs off as you swing your paddle, so you don't hit it very hard, but it gets the message. It swims away and disappears between two rocks near the Isibinia shore waving the white, segmented bone on the end of its tail as it goes. A rattle. It had a rattle?

"A swimming rattlesnake?" asks Danielle, flabbergasted. "I didn't know that those existed! I'll bet it was poisonous."

"Did it have fangs?" Dave asks.

"Yes," you remember. You are all a bit stunned.

"So you guys, what are we going to do now?" Dave is impatient as another rumble of thunder fills the air.

"The snake is still in this area," Danielle states professionally, "so we shouldn't get off here. We could get off on Isibinia Ndogo."

"Or we could just get off on another part of this island," Dave recommends hopefully.

"Where would you like to go?" Danielle asks you.

(If you would like to go to Isibinia Ndogo, go to page 45.)
(If you would like to try to land on another part of Isibinia itself, go to page 84.)

Back-paddle! You quickly begin to paddle in the opposite direction. You soon realize that not warning Dave and Danielle about the snake was a mistake. They are still paddling forward.

"What are you *doing?*" Danielle asks as your back-paddling turns the boat perpendicular to the shore. Then she sees it. The snake, still in the water, raises its head and rattled tail out of the water and stares her in the face with its cold, beady eyes. It lunges. Danielle reacts. She swings her paddle around. With a dull thud, the snake splashes back in the water and swims away, waving its rattled tail in the air. You and Dave back-paddle as fast as you can out of the bay.

"I'm sorry, Danny; I never thought…." Dave never knew that the islands housed snakes that large.

"We need to go home," Danielle interrupts, shivering from fear and the adrenaline rush. You and Dave look at each other, agree and then begin to paddle out of the channel. The island Isibinia to your left is blocking all the oncoming waves from the big part of the lake, so the going is fairly easy...at first.

You round the other side of the island to where the waves from the open lake are no longer blocked. The waves coming at you are over two feet high. All of you paddle furiously as the spray whips around you. Far off in the distance Lake Victoria seems to be flowing out of a gray sky. The wind whips around you, and the crash of a million waves creates a rumble like a continuous peal of thunder.

Being in the front of a canoe during a rising storm is quite an experience. The waves lift you up, pass below you and then drop you into their gullies. You and the front of the boat crash down in time to plow into the next blue mountain wave. You're getting wet and cold. Water pours over the front of the boat and sloshes around your feet. "How much water would it take to sink an aluminum canoe?" you wonder.

Dave yells something at you from the back of the boat. You turn around to try to hear him, only to have a wave douse your back. Danielle laughs against the wind but manages to pass along the message. "He says that you should come farther back in the boat and kneel down on the floor! It will stabilize the boat, and the nose of the canoe will ride higher so we won't get as wet."

"You mean you won't get as wet!" You're the one who has to kneel in inches of cold water and try to paddle awkwardly over the side of the boat. The worst part of it all is that you're not even halfway home yet. You paddle more and more, until your arms begin to ache. You look back at the others. They seem tired too. You dip the end of your paddle into the water and watch it drift backwards. Danielle says something about hot showers and cocoa at home, and you begin to paddle again. By now your muscles are burning.

Danielle yells through the storm, "We need to rest in shifts! You go first." You put down your paddle and feel the acid draining out of your muscles. Then you pick up your paddle again. Instantly Danielle puts hers down. In a few moments the boat begins to drift to the right. You paddle as hard as you can to counteract this movement. It's hard to steer a canoe from the front. You look at the back. Sure enough, Dave is the one resting. He looks at the new course of the canoe, groans and picks up his paddle again. With a few valiant heaves of his paddle, the canoe is back on course. It's your turn to rest. The land looks much closer. Now at least your arms have begun to go numb. Your nose and knees are numb, too, from cold wind and water.

Your thoughts get shorter and shorter. Lift the paddle, pull the paddle back. Lift the paddle, pull the paddle back. Switch sides. Lift the paddle, pull the paddle. You have given up watching the land. The water has gotten calmer. Six more violent pulls with the paddle and you're there! You jump out of the canoe and pull it partway up on the sand, then stand there on gelatin legs, waiting for Danielle and Dave to climb out of the boat. Danielle steps over the side of the boat as if it were a mountain ridge, then staggers uncertainly up the sandy bank.

Dave steps over the edge of the boat, looks around and falls down on the sand, laughing with relief. You and Danielle follow suit. The sand is full of soot, and all of you are wet, though Dave and Danielle didn't get as wet as you.

"I would kiss the ground if I didn't know what was in it," Dave says. You all agree. It feels wonderful to be back on solid ground. Even the loose sand feels solid now.

Within 3 minutes there are 30 Africans of all ages (you counted the number) standing around the three of you in a semicircle, looking on. Danielle stands up and shakes the sand off her long damp skirt. Her entire back is covered with black soot. "We need to drag the boat up the hill," she reminds you and Dave. You both groan.

Dave rolls over and tries to pull himself up with his arms but groans and falls back again. After much trouble, all three of you are out of the dirt and getting ready to drag the boat up the sandy embankment. No sooner have you begun than ten of the Africans lift the boat and begin to carry it with you. With their help, the boat seems almost to fly to the top of the hill, dragging the three of you with it. Dave and Danielle thank them as you reach the yard. They smile and walk away.

Aunt Debbie sends you into the shower first. Both she and Uncle Darryl are concerned that you had to kneel in lake water for 15 minutes. As soon as you get into the warm shower, you hear them lecturing Dave and Danielle. You catch the words *bilharzia* and *fluke*, accompanied by a lot of "buts" from Dave and Danielle. You don't hear another mention of it after getting out of the shower, but no one is in very high spirits. Dave in particular seems sullen and angry. Once you are all three showered and in dry clothes, you sit around in the living room drinking hot cocoa. You talk about the snake you saw (unidentifiable in the snake books) and about how your arms hurt (which they will continue to do for at least another day). You're dead tired, but you're proud that together, despite all odds, you made it home.

THE END

Without saying anything to Dave and Danielle, you walk off to the other end of valley. You reenter the lakeside trees and climb over rocks until you get to the lake. Rinsing your hand in the cool, dark water, you wonder why in the world Danielle and Dave are forbidden to touch it. It seems like an unnecessary precaution. Your rash certainly feels better now. You stand up and then hear a strange sound. It sounds like the bleating of a small sheep or goat.

(If you ignore the sound and go to find Dave and Danielle, go to page 91.)
(If you try to go and find the animal, go to page 115.)

Dave turns the boat parallel to the waves and you feel a wave of hopelessness. Danielle said that you would end up a mile farther down shore than you wanted to, but at this angle, it looks much farther. Suddenly, like a huge cradle, the boat slides sideways up and over a wave, threatening to dump its passengers.

"Balance!" Dave shouts as he begins to paddle. After a while you figure out how to move with the motion of the boat without allowing it to tip over. You never knew that your backbone was so flexible.

The good news is that the shore is coming up closer on the left. You have been concentrating on paddling for so long that you didn't notice your legs. They are beginning to feel strange and fidgety, as though you have been sitting in a car for the past three hours instead of a canoe. You haven't been able to stretch them at all and your arms have been working full time. You feel like jumping out of the boat, even right in the middle of the wavy water. "Turning in to shore!" Dave announces. Both you and Danielle begin paddling on the right side of the canoe to help him. You paddle as you never have before. You are making progress but the shore is farther away than it looked. Twenty minutes later, you ram the canoe onto a deserted beach with rocks and green bushes beyond. It feels odd to stand on solid ground again.

Danielle sits down on the sand and rests her elbows on her knees. Dave's arms are hanging at his sides like a rag doll's. He sits on a nearby boulder and flexes one arm only to double up in pain. "My biceps will never be the same again."

"Is that good?" Danielle looks up.

"Yup," Dave nods, flexing his expanded muscle more appreciatively. He winces and turns to you. "How are *your* arms?" You tell him.

"Mine are burning," Danielle moans, on the verge of tears. "There is no way that we're going to paddle home now!"

"I brought a padlock and chain," Dave reminds her. "We can hide the boat in the cornfield, chain it to that mango tree just in case anyone finds it, and then walk home." You look behind you and see a large mango tree far out in the rows of corn behind the bushes.

"I can't do anything right now. Let's just wait a minute." Danielle falls back wearily on the sand. You all stay put for a few minutes, watching white egrets wading and fishing by the beach.

"Danny," Dave rouses her, "the sun is beginning to go down. We don't have much time. Two hours from now it will be dark and the mosquitoes will be coming out."

"Just what I need! Another case of malaria." Danielle sits up and buries her head wearily in her arms.

Dave whispers to you, "Danielle had malaria about four months ago. That disease is the biggest killer around here. Well, maybe not." He reconsiders. "Bilharzia is pretty bad, too."

"What about AIDS?" you ask.

"Malaria is a killer comparable with AIDS. It's hard to find a family that hasn't lost someone to malaria," Dave tells you. "AIDS eats your white blood cells, but malaria eats the red ones, so it kills a lot faster. Babies don't survive malaria if they are not treated immediately because they don't have very much blood. Danielle was really healthy when she got malaria. After a week of the disease, it took her *six weeks* to get her strength back. That one week of malaria was pretty bad. She had fevers over 104 degrees, excruciating headaches…. She got overdosed on one kind of medicine, so…."

"What are you guys talking about?" Danielle wants to know.

"I was just talking about that night you started yelling at Mom to take the necklace out of your mouth because of the pink sheep…."

"I didn't say that!"

"Dad was on a trip then, so he missed the whole thing," Dave continues. "So then, once Danny stopped talking gibberish, she said that she had too much energy…."

"Yeah," Danielle seems bored. "And then I kicked my throw-up bowl off the bed…."

"It went flying!" Dave adds gleefully.

"Dave, you love this story, don't you? Next time why don't you ask me before you tell my embarrassing malaria stories? It wasn't my fault!"

"I know, but can't I tell the next part? Danny said that she had an uncontrollable urge to rip something; so Mom gave her a cardboard box to tear up, you know, one of those big packing boxes, and Danny just ripped it to bits! I've never seen her so violent!"

"I told you that I had too much energy. Anyway, after that the medicine wore off, and I was back in my right mind. Shall we go, you guys?" Danielle finishes.

"Sure." The three of you drag the canoe through the furrows in the cornfield and padlock it to the mango tree. You cover it with some brush and then begin walking.

The little paths through the cornfields have been packed down, hard and narrow. You follow them, heading in the general direction of home as much as you can. When you finally reach a road, Dave recognizes it and sighs with relief.

"I've ridden my bike out here. If we just follow it that way…." You pass many African homes. Most have mud walls and grass roofs. Some have metal roofs. The larger houses are about eight by ten feet. Often people call out to you.

Danielle and Dave greet them. "*Shikamo.*" Danielle curtseys with every greeting she gives. Some of the small children greet you.

You learn the reply, *Marahaba*. You find out from Dave and Danielle what it means. *Shikamo* means, "I grab your feet." *Marahaba* means, "Do it a few times." No grabbing of feet actually takes place.

One lady runs out from a house carrying a little booklet. Dave and Danielle are quite interested since it is one of the materials that the translators and their dad produced. "See?" Danielle shows you. "Psalm 23!"

"The illustrations were done by the son of one of the translators," Dave tells you. "Hey, Danielle, ask her where she got it."

"From an Mzinza literacy teacher who was going door to door in Mwangika," Danielle finds out. "She was visiting her sister there."

The woman begins talking rapidly. Danielle translates. "She said that the concept of having a meal with your enemy is really radical around here."

"What are you talking about?" Dave questions. "The psalm says that God prepared a table in the 'sight' of the enemy. That doesn't necessarily mean that the enemy eats it with you."

"In Africa it probably does," Danielle decides. "You never eat in the sight of anyone without inviting them to eat with you."

"What are we talking about? We've got to get going!" Dave replaces his cap.

Every time someone calls out from a house on the side of the road, David and Danielle have to greet or be greeted by everyone in sight, introduce you and decline a fervent invitation to dinner. This is the wrong time of day to attempt a quick walk home. Everyone is getting ready to eat. Danielle explains in Kiswahili that, No, you can't stay for dinner. Her parents are worried and you must get home. Dave and Danielle tear themselves away from one gracious invitation after another.

"That last family was having cooked bananas for dinner!" Danielle sighs longingly. "It even smelled like the sweet kind! I love those."

"We have four general types of bananas here," Dave explains to you. "And two of them are meant to be cooked." Another person calls out from the side of the road. Danielle groans. Dave grins.

"Nothing like African hospitality."

"You do the talking this time, Dave!" Danielle insists.

"You're the one who speaks the language," Dave replies, grinning.

"You know enough," Danielle says darkly.

"Believe me, with my Kiswahili, refusing a dinner invitation would take a lot longer." He sniffs the air. "And if that family really is having *chapatis*, I might just end up saying the wrong thing and then we'll have to stay for dinner!"

"Come on, Dave! I've been rude six times already!" Danielle turns toward the yard with a curtsey. *"Shikamo!"*

"Why can't we just say, 'Sorry, can't stop in, have to get home,' and skip the whole greeting process?" you ask Dave.

"It is unthinkable," Dave says simply. "Refusing an invitation of hospitality isn't polite, but not stopping to greet someone is like spitting in their face!"

After the ninth dinner invitation, you reach the missionaries' long driveway. You all begin to run. Simba barks as you approach the house but then comes up wagging her tail.

Aunt Debbie meets you on the back porch. "You're back! What happened?" she asks.

"We went so far out into the lake that we got washed way down the shoreline," Danielle explains.

"So we chained up the boat in a cornfield and walked home," Dave finishes.

"Your dad and I were really worried about all of you. He took the motorboat out to look for you."

"I'll take a flashlight and go signal to him from the shore," Dave suggests. "Then he and I can go pick up the canoe."

"Not tonight," Aunt Debbie puts her foot down. "Put on a jacket and go signal to your dad, then come back here. The rest of us are going to eat dinner. The food is getting cold. Besides, it's time for the radio call."

"What's for dinner?" Dave asks excitedly.

"Cooking bananas. They were a gift from Mama Joseph."

Danielle sighs happily. Dave looks disappointed.

"We'll be having tacos tomorrow after I get ground beef from the market," Aunt Debbie reassures him. "Actually, since they're made with *chapatis* and not tortillas, they're probably the same as 'wraps' in the United States."

"All right!" Dave grabs a flashlight and heads out the door.

The End

The sun has come out and the shade of the big tree looks cool and inviting.

"Let's stay on this island," you say as you glance around.

Dave nods in approval and steps off toward the path. At that moment you hear the sound of two very large animals scurrying away from you. The one immediately off to the right was very close! You get a good view of the other one. It was a lizard, four or five feet long. It crawled out from under a flower bush in the direction of the smallest island. Danielle freezes in place.

"See what I meant, Danielle?" Dave says, waving her on. "They *always* run away from us!"

You seem to have come to the end of the forest. The trees stop directly ahead of you. Dead vines cover the ground.

"I think these vines have snakeweed," Danielle says, kneeling down to look at them. "It's a shame when a parasite gets loose on this island. It kills everything."

"*Snake*weed?" You don't like the sound of that.

"I think they call it snakeweed because it snakes around," Danielle decides. "All the same, we should watch our step." You continue following the path, now only a compression in the weeds.

"Look, you guys!" Danielle darts off to the side. What looked like a rise in the land is actually a small shelter. Someone has propped up a section of the snakeweed carpet with sticks, creating a lean-to type of shelter. Danielle crawls inside and sits up; Dave follows her. The house is too small for a third person, so you wait your turn outside. Once inside, you are shaded from the sun, but the house wouldn't keep out rain. Maybe someone built it just for fun.

You all keep going. The path continues to the top of the hill and then turns right. Now that you are on the top of the island, you can see the lake on four sides. You walk over campfire ashes, more evidence of the presence of man on this piece of "wilderness." You come to a fork in the path. The straight path seems to lead right back to the blinding white rocky shore, but the other fork dives off to the right and disappears into….

"House Veg!" Danielle coos, with a glint in her eyes. You look. All you can see is a wall of leaves, as tall as a small house. "I've always wondered what it looks like inside one of those!"

"Danny," Dave warns, "*kenges* like to sit inside the House Veg, especially during the hot parts of the day—like right now. And you don't like them, remember?"

Standing on top of the hill in the brilliant equatorial sunlight makes the leafy vegetation below seem welcoming. Then again, any monitor lizard could have the same thought. Danielle's eyes are sparkling with adventure. You see a family resemblance as Danielle's curiosity comes to light.

"Danielle," Dave uses her full name for emphasis, "it's one thing to get off on a monitor lizard's island; it is another to walk right into their living rooms."

"As you said before, Dave, monitor lizards always run away. I've just always wanted to see what it looks like inside a House Veg."

"What do *you* think?" Dave asks you. *Say no!* he mouths.

(If you want to enter the House Vegetation, go to page 97.)
(If you decide to take the other fork of the path to the rocky shoreline, go to page 101.)

"I'd like to try to go to Isibinia Ndogo Sana," you decide.

"Well, off we go then," Dave says resignedly. "Lead the way, Danny." No sooner have you started in that direction than a huge monitor lizard crawls out from under a flower bush, crosses the path and disappears again. It had the head of a lizard but the body of an alligator.

"Why don't you lead the way?" Danielle ducks behind Dave and pushes him ahead of her.

"Okay, okay," Dave says. You can't help but notice the back of his neck turning a shade paler under the sweat.

"Here's where we get our feet wet," Dave announces grimly. The small island is just ahead, across a ten-foot section of water with scattered rocks that form the isthmus between the two islands.

"*Maybe* I can jump this," Dave mumbles to himself. He steps back, then tries a valiant leap across the water toward a large pointed rock. His foot slips off the rock and splashes into the water, soaking his shoe. He reaches out and grabs the rock with both hands, lifts his wet shoe and shakes off the water. "I doubt that any bilharzia could have gotten to me in that short amount of time." He hops to another rock. One more leap puts him onto Isibinia Ndogo Sana. Danielle is busy rearranging rocks near the shoreline so she won't have to jump as far.

This island is about 30 feet long and 15 feet wide. Tall dry grass, some with sharp pointy balls growing on the tops of the stems, is everywhere. You walk uncertainly, trying to avoid twisting an ankle on the loose rocks below the weeds.

"Look!" Danielle shouts excitedly, running down to the shore of Isibinia Ndogo Sana to stand under the island's small, lone tree. She pauses to survey a chunk of granite. It is a large rock, two feet across and a foot tall with a hollow top. The rock is placed almost exactly at the waterline, so the hollow must have been formed from centuries of water flowing in and out of it. "I've been wanting to get a birdbath for the yard," she explains. "This is perfect!"

Dave steps down with an engineer's stride to inspect the rock. He gives his assessment. "Danny, it's huge."

"Well," she continues, not defeated, "if we go back, get the canoe and bring it around to this side of the island, the three of us should be able to lift the rock into the boat. Then we can paddle it home."

Dave is surveying the rock on all sides. He tries to tilt it on its side to look at the bottom but discovers that it's too heavy. "What are you doing, Dave?" Danielle asks.

"Looking for sharp points that might puncture the aluminum of the canoe when we drop this two-hundred-pound rock into it."

"There *are* three of us," you remind him. "We can *lower* it into the boat, right?"

"I suppose," Dave agrees. Danielle smiles.

When Dave finally comes paddling around the far tip of the island, his whole side has obviously been doused in water. "I took a spill crossing back to Isibinia Ndogo. Let's get this rock in quickly. I need to go home and take a shower."

The three of you decide to take the rock lifting in two stages. First, you will heave it up onto the edge of the canoe. Then after a rest you will lower it down to the floor of the canoe. You and Dave each put one foot into the boat to steady it. Then you all lift and strain until the rock is finally resting precariously on the side of the canoe. You rest and then begin stage two. You are surprised at the force of gravity. "Your feet!" shrieks Danielle as the rock crashes down. You get them out of the way just in time.

You survey the boat for holes, then get in and paddle back around the small island. "Shhhhh!" Dave says from the back of the boat. You have come upon flocks and flocks of black birds and white birds standing by the shore, each about a foot tall. Some are busy holding up their wings to dry them; some are fishing, and others are just looking around.

"One, two, three…." Dave whispers. Dave and Danielle are both holding their paddles over the boat. A bird cries out in alarm.

"Go!" Danielle shouts, and she and Dave begin banging their paddles on the edges of the boat as loud as they can. The noise is deafening, and all 200 birds, black cormorants and white egrets, take to flight. The sight of 200 sets of wings rising up in perfect, rustling formation is spectacular. The beating sounds of the wings die away as the birds relocate to the other side of Isibinia.

The extra weight makes the trip home more difficult, but that is nothing compared to the trouble it takes to pull the canoe up the embankment with a two-hundred-pound rock in it. After dumping the rock out of the boat, you decide to leave it there overnight.

The next day the three of you begin the construction of this rustic addition to the front yard. You find smaller, six-inch, rocks and build a pillar. Then you lift the rock to the top. Dave knows how to do a

cement mix, so you ask Uncle Darryl for some cement and mix it with water and gray beach sand. You all pile it on the sides of the rock to make the side higher and the hollow deeper. It has to dry for another day before you can fill it with water. Uncle Darryl and Aunt Debbie are delighted with the addition to their yard and the brightly colored birds that flock to it within minutes, but the birdbath's biggest fan is the cat.

The End

You still want to try to get off on Isibinia; after all, it is the biggest island.

"Let's try to land somewhere else on this island," you decide.

Keeping Isibinia Island on your right, you all paddle away from the beach and down the channel between it and the other islands, hoping to stop at another landing point which Dave says will put you closer to the region of the caves. You are not expecting the storm that you meet at the other end of the channel. Maybe it would have been better to walk across the island, but that snake left you without options. Paddling against two-foot waves is no picnic.

"Turn in here!" Dave alerts the two of you from the back of the boat. This is not an easy feat because you and Danielle have your backs to him, and the wind from the head-on storm is blowing his words the other way. Finally you hear him and both paddle on the left side to help him out as he steers the boat into a sheltered cove under a large overhanging tree. This side of the island has quite a few more trees. Vines are hanging everywhere, and moss and ferns cover the ground between the rocks. Looking down into the water, you spot a very sharp jagged rock just under the surface. You quickly jab your paddle at it and push the boat away. The rock's jagged tip showed evidence of another boat's paint.

"Wow! That was close!" Danielle is staring at the rock's jagged tip. "Some other boat (painted white) must have hit that rock some time in the past! And that one." She notices a rock closer to the shore that is sticking out of the water about six inches. Its upper jagged ridge is coated in aluminum scraping. "Dave?" Danielle gives him a sly look.

"That must have been the rock that I hit when I came out here with my friends last rainy season," Dave clarifies for her. "The water was higher then, and I couldn't see that rock because it was so dark. Now, of course," he eyes the glittering beacon, "anyone could see it."

The three of you drag the boat up a very steep incline of rocks, where Dave chains it to a tree. Then you all stash your life jackets behind a rock. You don't think that anyone will look for them, if anyone stops by before you all get back. But "Better safe than sorry," as they say. "Now off to the caves," Dave says brightly.

"I did have one other idea," Danielle suggests. "I thought that we could go look the storm in the face."

Dave looks amused. "I thought we got out of the water so that we wouldn't *have* to do that."

Danielle explains hurriedly, "If we follow the shore, it will take us to the far point of the island. There is a rock there, a little way out in the water. That side of the island faces the open lake, and that is where the storm is coming from, so that's the part of the island where the storm will hit the hardest. If we go over there, we'll be able to sit on the rock with the waves crashing at us, and the wind blowing, and lightning out in the distance over the lake going as far away as the eye can see…. I just think it would be a really neat place to go."

"Hmmm." Dave slouches. "I don't know about going out to sit on a rock during a lightning storm."

"We don't actually have to sit on the rock. We can just watch the storm from that general area."

"Okay," Dave agrees, "I would come with you, but since this is probably the only time our guest will be on these islands…." He turns to you. "Just in case you've had your heart set on going to the caves, I'll ask you. Where would you rather go?"

(If you would like to go "look the storm in the face," go to page 148.)
(If you would like to visit the caves, go to page 155.)

"Hi ho! Hi ho. It's to the caves we go!" Dave starts whistling the next part of the familiar tune from *Snow White and the Seven Dwarfs* as he hikes up the hill.

"Dave, you're such a goofball!" Danielle comments in the middle of his performance as she struggles up the hill behind him. Dave doesn't miss a beat and continues to sing.

"I know! I know, I know, I know. Hi ho, it's to the caves we go!" Even Danielle has to smile. "This is fun!" Dave is hopping from rock to rock, thoroughly enjoying himself.

The path winds off to the left around the side of the hill. Danielle is about to take the path to the side. "Danielle, remember what we said," Dave reminds her. "We're going to go right over the middle of the island to the caves."

"You guys can keep going up the hill. I'll take the path. It probably leads to the caves anyway. Don't worry; I'll be within shouting distance. I'll probably get there first." Danielle disappears around the corner and out of sight.

"No." Dave pauses, one foot resting on a boulder. "If Danielle takes the path, she'll probably end up by the lake and have to retrace her steps. We're the ones who are going to get there first. Come on!" He takes off running up the hill. You follow. Jumping like a goat from large rock to large rock is easier than having to meander through the boulders. Dave has stopped up ahead, panting. "Once we get to the top of the hill," he says between breaths, "we should be able to spot Danielle and the caves. We'll know which way to go and how far ahead she is."

"I thought that you were confident that we would get to the caves first," you remind him.

"I didn't take it into account the fact that we are climbing a mountain and battling the wild, while she is strolling down an easy path. But who cares? This will be more fun. At least it will be more interesting," he comments, rubbing a scratched elbow. You finally reach the small shade tree at the top of the mountain. A very loud rustling noise startles both of you. Two large brown, perfectly camouflaged birds appear out of nowhere and take flight from among the dry round leaves on the ground. They are gone in an instant. Dave slaps his leg. "I just wasn't fast enough." He's busy putting a small Y-shaped slingshot, with a long rubber strip tied between its ends, back into his pocket.

You step back out into the sun, which has begun to shine again, and then take a look around. You can see the lake off to your left as well as stretching out above the trees on your right. You can't see Danielle; the island is covered in trees and dry bushes. You both listen for a moment and then, "Danny!" Dave shouts. You listen for a reply. There is none. "Let's try together," Dave suggests. "One, two, three...."

"Daaaaaaanny!" you both shout. Not even an echo greets your words. "I think she would respond if she could hear us." Dave decides, "Maybe she has made it to the caves already. Let's keep going."

You and Dave weave your way through very dry prickly bushes. When you finally reach an open space on the way down the hill, you find it to be completely populated by snake holes. You and Dave cross it gingerly and then reenter the brush on the other side. The bracken is composed of scratchy, twiggy bushes. Neither of you has a *panga* (brush slasher) with you, so the going is hard. You squeeze through where you can, but you seem to be drifting off to the right, away from the caves and especially from Danielle.

"At last!" Dave sighs in relief as you break through the bracken and come face to face with two gigantic rocks. "A lookout point. If we can get up there, we'll know how to get out of this mess." You and Dave circle the rocks, looking for a way to climb them. Your best bet seems to be one eight-foot side of the smaller boulder. All the other sides of the rocks are taller.

"One of us is going to have to be a ladder, or we'll never get up there," Dave says, assessing the vertical slope. "So which would you rather be? The climber or the foot-holder?"

(If you'd rather be the climber, go to page 108.)
(If you'd rather be the foot-holder, go to page 118.)

Whatever that sound is, you don't want to be bothered by it. Dave and Danielle will have missed you by now. You run back into the valley, climb the hill, and hear their voices as well as some others down the other side of the cliff. You peer over the side to see Dave talking with two African boys and one man by the waterline. You're back at the lake. Danielle notices you. "Come down! Dave's friends from the Luo fishing camp can give us a ride back to our boat!" Danielle must be ignoring your disappearance.

"So where were you?" Dave asks you.

"Dave, don't ask," Danielle cautions.

"Why?" Dave asks her, then, "Oh, yeah."

"Where did you think I was?" you ask, climbing around washed-out rock formations that have created caves here and there.

"Well, when someone disappears for a short time, we usually assume that they've...." she pauses.

"Gone to the bathroom," Dave finishes with a roll of his eyes. "Of course, there are no bathrooms on these islands, but when necessity calls…."

"Ahem?" says Danielle.

You meet Pita and Ezekieli and their father. Pita and Ezekieli are the boys' baptismal names, the Kiswahili equivalents of Peter and Ezekiel. They are of the Luo tribe.

African wooden canoes are interesting to ride in. This one is much bigger than the aluminum canoe. The bottom is always filled with water. Someone bails it out periodically, using a three-liter corn oil jug with the top cut off. Dave picks up a paddle and joins in the rhythmic precision paddling of his African friends. Ezekieli asks Dave a question. "What did he say, Dave?" you want to know.

"He asked why Danielle is wearing my hat." Dave answers him. Then Pita asks a question. Ezekieli leans forward eagerly. Dave answers in the affirmative.

"And that time?" you ask again.

"Oh, he just wanted to know if we're going to be showing any more movies again anytime soon. A few months back we showed our friends the *JESUS* film in Kiswahili at our house. We'll be showing it up at the church on New Year's Eve. Just think," he pauses, "in a few more years we'll have the book of Luke translated into Kizinza. Then they can dub Kizinza into the *JESUS* film too! That'll be cool."

"Yeah, it will probably be the first Kizinza movie ever," Danielle agrees.

When you finally get back to the canoe, Dave's friends stop the boat and wait for him to get out. Dave, with the help of Danielle, tries to explain that he'd like them to paddle their boat closer to the shore so that you can all get out and get the canoe without getting wet. You know that you have already touched the water and keep quiet. Finally they pull up to the shore. You all get out on shore and say good-bye to the three laughing Africans. They think it is incredibly funny that the foreigners are so afraid of getting wet. Dave goes and unchains the canoe, red-faced and angry.

"It isn't that I'm such a wimp and I can't stand to touch the water! I was on a swim team before I came to Africa. But they don't understand. Besides, I could outswim them any day."

"That's because they probably can't swim at all," Danielle clarifies.

"Right," Dave agrees.

You know that there's something you need to mention, but you aren't sure if you want to. "You guys," you ask, "is it guaranteed that someone will get bilharzia every time that they touch the water?"

"Well…no," Dave is putting the chain down into the canoe, "but there is always a chance, and the chance gets greater the longer you stay in. If you go swimming, you're guaranteed to get it, especially if you go swimming near the shore. That's where the bilharzia concentration is the greatest. Some people just don't care."

Danielle is giving you a strange look. "Did you fall in or something? You can get tested for it if you think there's a chance that you might have it." Dave tosses you a life jacket.

You know that you only put your hands into the water for a very short time, so you might get off easy. You could tell Dave and Danielle, or you could get tested, or you could just forget about it. You made the decision to wash off the rash, and the water did help it. You won't know the consequences of washing in the water until much later.

THE END

"Let's go to the Shelf," you decide.

The three of you start off to the side of the clearing, detecting stepping rocks under the dry vines and grass that covers the ground. After pushing through some tree branches, you reach the rocky shoreline. You climb over and around wobbly sharp rocks but soon have to turn inland again because of an overhanging tree. Then you find yourselves caught in a mess of trees and wet vines as you try to get back to the shoreline. "Let's just keep as close to the shore as possible," Dave suggests, resignedly heading inland again.

Suddenly Danielle stops dead in her tracks in front of you. "Be quiet!" she whispers fearfully. At first all that you hear is Dave crunching through dead sticks up ahead. Then you hear another sound, coming from the other direction. Something very heavy is coming toward you. In fact, a whole herd of some-things. They're coming up fast and they're not slow-ing down.

(If you climb a tree, go to page 124.)
(If you run in the other direction, go to page 131.)

Why not look inside? you think to yourself. *Just one look isn't going to hurt anybody.* "Why not?" you voice your opinion. Dave groans.

"Let's go!" Danielle skips down the path and directly into the House Veg. You are about to follow when there is a loud shriek. Danielle comes shooting back up the path. She glances quickly behind her and trips on a protruding rock. Dave catches her arm on her way over and then pulls her back up. She totters and then sits down on a nearby rock, holding her big toe through her shoe. "I think I broke it."

You count seven distinct splashes of large animals entering the water at full speed. Dave chuckles, "You sure know how to find them!"

Danielle is busy taking off her shoe. The end of her toenail is smashed and her toe is badly bruised, but the bones seem to be okay. Dave sighs, "Let's go home, Danny. You probably need to put your foot on ice." Danielle grimaces.

You have another idea. "Now that we've scared all the monitors out of there, we should at least go and check out the House Veg."

"That sounds like a good idea," Danielle agrees, carefully putting her sock back on, "but you go first this time."

You agree. "Ouch!" Danielle shrieks in pain as she attempts to put her shoe back on. "I give up. It's no use." She drops her shoe hopelessly on the ground. "These shoes were already a bit small."

"Allow me," says Dave, coming back and gallantly offering her his arm. She picks up her shoe with one hand, takes his arm with the grandeur of a queen, and then giggles as she begins hopping clumsily after you in the direction of the House Veg.

What you find as you enter is a typical rocky beach. A sideways tree trunk is lying across the center of it with many tall and thin branches sticking up to the roof. The leaves on the tangled mess of branches shade the area. If you were a monitor lizard, you would live here. *And if you were a snake!* you realize with a start. Just ahead, draped across the rocks, is a gigantic snake skeleton.

"Look what I found!" you hear from behind you. "Clothes!" Danielle is excitedly pulling a red shirt and a pair of old black pants from under a rock, where they had been carefully stashed. "Obviously someone else lives in here."

"Or stashes their clothes in here," Dave replies.

"Ouch!" Danielle sits down hard, clutching her toe in agony, the pants thrown over her lap.

"Danielle, if you're going to keep bumping that, we need to go home." Dave is busy stashing the shirt back under the rock.

"You guys, you better come look at this!" you call out, keeping an eye on the skeleton. Danielle is using the branches around her to stand up. "What *is* that?"

Dave crawls over to you and stops with his mouth hanging open. "That's over ten feet!" he gasps.

"Let's measure it, you guys! Ouch!" Danielle stubs her toe in her excitement to get over to it.

You break off a stick about a foot in length and begin measuring the skeleton. Seventeen feet long! "Are you sure that stick is a foot long?" Danielle asks.

"We can take it back home with us and measure it," Dave decides.

"The skeleton? We'd break it!" Danielle is horrified.

"No, the stick," Dave corrects.

The going is slow back across the island with one lame person. Dave and Danielle want to bring their parents back to see the snake. "Supposedly all the pythons died out in Kahunda years ago!" Danielle says, as she hops beside Dave, carrying one shoe.

"Maybe that was the last one," Dave hypothesizes.

The stormy weather has cleared up completely by the time you get back to the canoe. When you get home, Danielle is exempted from having to pull the canoe up the beach; instead Uncle Darryl leaves his computer translation work to come down and help.

In measuring the stick, you find out the snake must have been approaching 18 feet long. Uncle Darryl insists that you take him the next time you go.

Danielle spends the evening watching TV with her toe bandaged and propped on a pillow.

THE END

"Let's keep going." You agree with Dave about the House Veg. Even though you and Dave are going to follow the path down to the lake, Danielle still insists on taking at least a peek inside, just to see what it looks like. As she peers inside and the sound of many bulky, scurrying animals meets your ears, you know what is in there. Danielle runs back, nervous, eager to get away.

"It was really neat, though," she tells you. "Just like a house, with columns of branches holding up the leaves...."

You have reached the shore, and all of you are stumbling around on blinding white, wobbly rocks. You can see Isibinia across the channel, so you know that the boat is nearby. Then you realize that the white thing ahead of you is not a rock. You move closer. It is a skull. It looks like a monitor lizard skull. It's the size of *your* head, though longer and narrower.

"That was one good-sized granddaddy," Dave says, coming up.

Danielle approaches it cautiously. You notice her discreetly trying to sniff the air around it as she bends down for a closer look. "Dave," she says brightly, "maybe you could take this home and replace your cow skull! It's getting so old, and the bones are full of bugs and," she adds quietly, "it smells rotten. Besides," she returns to her normal tone of voice, "a monitor lizard skull is so much more rare!"

"Well, actually, Danny, I didn't see it first. Our guest did but," he turns to you, "if you don't want it, I'll add it to my collection."

"Collection?" Danielle looks horrified. "Isn't one piece of dead animal enough for you? Your room smells horrible already!"

"Danny, that's just the way my room always smells. I don't think that one old cow skull makes a huge difference. I don't have a collection of skulls yet, but I could start one. I'll get a bird skull, a goat skull…."

"Why does my bedroom have to be next door to yours? I'll have to smell this collection too!"

"I'll get Mom and Dad to move your bedroom to the other end of the house."

"Ha, ha." Danielle looks crestfallen. "My room already shares a wall with the bathroom, which

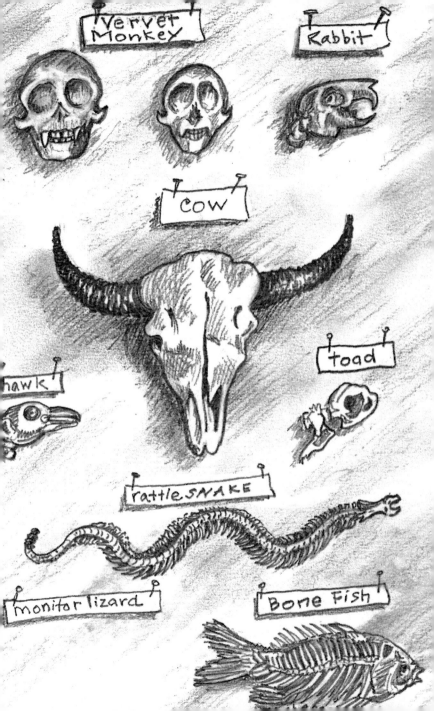

doesn't smell very good. Couldn't you keep all your animal skulls out in the yard where they belong?"

"The last time we discussed this, you said that I should give my cow skull a proper *burial* out in the yard."

"I still think that."

"You have stumbled upon one of the issues in which my sister and I strongly disagree," Dave remarks sadly to you.

"That's right," Danielle affirms.

(If you would like to take the skull for yourself, go to page 136.)
(If you would rather leave it and let Dave and Danielle work it out, go to page 137.)

You startle backwards and fling the worm out of your hand and over the side of the boat. At that moment, a wave hits. You feel yourself falling backwards and then hit cool water. Your feet touch the squishy soupy mud floor of the lake for a moment just before your life jacket pulls you to a firm floating position. Danielle is staring down at you, dumbfounded. Dave is trying very hard not to laugh. A wave washes into your mouth as you try to speak. Lake Victoria is the most disgusting thing you have ever tasted. It tastes like a combination of urine and vomit.

"Quick!" says Danielle. "Get out of the water! The longer you stay in it, the more chance you have of getting sick!"

You try to pull yourself over the edge of the boat, but sopping wet blue jeans are heavy and you feel like you might tip the boat over, so you swim to the shore. You slosh up the sandy beach and stand there, bedraggled, as Dave and Danielle paddle toward you. When they reach the shore, Dave roars with laughter.

"Dave!" Danielle reprimands, "This isn't really that funny! We need to take our guest home for a shower to wash off the water before the bilharzia burrows in."

"I'm sorry that I handed you the piece of worm"; Dave says between laughs, "it's just that you seemed so brave before. I didn't think that handing you a worm would make you fall out of the boat!" He continues chuckling.

"Dave, shame on you!" Danielle reprimands him, trying to hide a grin as he begins to laugh harder. She turns to you. "Let's walk home. Dave can paddle the boat back by himself as well as get his giggles out." Dave stops laughing and paddles himself away from the beach, but as you walk on, you can see Dave rounding the point, still laughing.

"So, Danielle," you ask, "I fell in the water and even drank some of it. What does that really mean?"

"It means that you have a good chance of getting sick," she says matter-of-factly. "Taking a shower before the water has a chance of drying on your skin is a way of decreasing your bilharzia chances. Of course, you could also get typhoid from drinking the water. Have you ever been immunized?" She doesn't let you answer. "We haven't had an epidemic of cholera for a long time, so you probably won't get that."

You can't believe it. Here is your friend listing off deadly diseases as if they were choices of breakfast cereal. "But don't worry," she tells you. *Uh huh*. "We'll keep an eye on you, and make sure you get tested for bilharzia in a few months."

You throw up as soon as you get into their house, which Aunt Debbie says is a very good thing. Whatever you got into your system, it's out now (on the family's cement floor). You were kind enough to avoid the throw rugs. When Dave arrives, he isn't laughing any more but is genuinely concerned about your welfare.

You end up getting a bad case of diarrhea, which, as Danielle says, you could have contracted *anywhere*, though the lake is a great place to find it. When you are tested a month later for bilharzia, you didn't get that either. You are glad.

THE END

Dave leans hard against the rock, locks his fingers together and then holds them out like a hammock, palms up. "Step into my hands," he commands. You lift your dirty dusty shoe and step into his grip. "Wait a minute!" Dave drops your foot and looks at his hand and then shrugs. "There was something damp and cold on the bottom of your shoe." You quickly check the bottom of your shoe and then scrape off some slimy black mud on the sharp ridge of a rock on the ground. "Don't bother." Dave locks his fingers again. "I've got enough of whatever-it-is on my hands already." You put one shoe into Dave's hand sling and hoist your weight up onto that foot, balancing with your hands against the rock. Now you can see over the top of the rock, but there isn't anything to grab onto to pull yourself up the rest of the way. Dave has begun to lift you. You fling yourself stomach down across the rock and then orient yourself into a kneeling position. You stand up. You can't really see anything. To your right is the shoreline. You and Dave are off course.

"So where are we?" Dave calls up.

"I don't know. The lake is just beyond those trees off to the right."

Dave slaps his knee and groans, "The lake should be on the left!"

Just then you see something soar and then plummet just over the tops of the trees to the left. You look closely. Then it happens again. A stick appears momentarily over the branches of the bracken before falling back to the ground. Then another. "Dave, someone's throwing sticks up in the air over there."

"Huh?" Dave squints up at you. "Uh. Oh, probably just some *kuni* collectors."

"What?"

"*Kuni* collectors are people who come to these islands to chop firewood illegally," Dave explains. Another stick flies straight up into the air, higher this time.

So if they're doing something illegal, why are they throwing sticks of firewood up into the air where they can be seen? Unless it's a signal.

"Dave, I think that someone is throwing sticks up the air to try to get our attention," you call down to him. "It might be Danielle."

Dave's ears perk up. "Danielle is throwing sticks up in the air? Or someone is. I'm going to go check it out. Direct me."

Dave cannot see the flying sticks from the ground, so you give him directions as he fights his way through twigs and thorns. You wait. After a while he reappears…with Danielle. The three of you, reunited, start off across the island to try to get back on course.

"So, Danny, did you make it to the caves?" Dave asks.

"No, I walked for a while and then went looking for you two."

"Why?"

Danielle explains, "I hadn't seen or heard anything of you guys for the past half-hour. I'd seen three *kenges,* though. They don't run away as quickly when I'm the only one coming. Being lost in the wilds by yourself may make a great movie, but I didn't enjoy it."

You are following the front shoreline of the island. This shore is tall and cliff-like. You can see the missionaries' house across the water. The island terrain has gone from brush to ground covered in grass and rocks. You can tell from the goat droppings littered everywhere that they love this area.

Then you hear an exclamation from Dave. He has run on ahead. You hurry to the edge of the hill and find yourself looking down a very steep incline, studded with large rocks with the lake at the bottom. As you climb down, you discover that you've made it to the caves.

There are several caves here, probably made by rain washing the dirt down the slope, leaving the rocks to stand piled on their own. Danielle and Dave have each found a cave to inspect. You decide to explore one just above the water. It seems to be a pretty good size. You look inside—straight into the eyes of a gigantic lizard. You dash back. As soon as you are out of the doorway, the lizard vacates its residence and escapes into the water. Danielle looks out of a cave just above and off to your right. "I think I've found the goat cave!" You climb up into Danielle's cave and then notice that the floor is covered with small round droppings. It's the goat cave, all right.

"A monitor lizard lives down in another one," you tell her.

"I hate to bring this up, you guys," Dave calls to you, "but we're supposed to be on our way home in 20 minutes."

"But it took us an hour to get here!" Danielle hurries out of the cave so quickly that she almost forgets that the land drops off directly outside of it.

"There were a few delays," Dave counters. "If we go back the way we came, we won't have to fight bracken this time, so it'll go faster."

"Well, let's go." You don't feel like pushing through any more scratchy bushes and twigs and getting any more weed seeds fastened to your clothes than are already there. You know that you have to get back to the boat. The brush will be easier the second time through.

"Of course, we *could* go my way back," Danielle says nonchalantly.

"Lead the way."

When you reach the boat, the day has turned into evening. You paddle home over orange-colored water, much calmer this time. You finally pull the canoe up the embankment, exhausted and scratched but happy. Aunt Debbie is waiting for you on the front porch.

"Sorry we're late, Mom; can I have a soda?" Dave asks his mother as the three of you carry your life jackets and paddles into the storeroom. She's standing on the back porch.

"You can all have sodas with dinner. It's ready."

"Where did Dad go?" Danielle asks.

"Dad? Go? Oh, yeah, the car's gone," says Dave, realizing that something very large and red just happens to be missing from their driveway.

"He went to Sengerema," Aunt Debbie says as you all go inside.

"What was it this time?" Dave asks, getting a cold soda bottle out of the bottom of the propane fridge.

"A woman was vomiting blood. Dad's taking her to Sengerema to get a blood transfusion. Her brother went along to be a blood donor since he's the most likely to have a compatible blood type."

"I didn't say good-bye," says Danielle quietly. She sees you looking at her. "Oh, Dad'll be back by tomorrow morning. It only takes four hours to get to Sengerema. Unfortunately, people usually come *after dark* to ask for rides. I know my dad is doing the right thing by driving, but the roads are so bad...." She pauses and then continues, "I always worry that he won't come home. I pray. I know that there are people in other places, like our home churches in America, praying for us. People should depend on God all the time everywhere, I guess, but *here* it seems like there's no one or nothing *else* to depend on. Maybe that's a good thing, but it sure takes the romance out of trusting God. It's cool, though, 'cause He does take care of us. At least, most of the time. Sometimes I really wonder what He's up to. Trusting God is so hard." She looks up, embarrassed. "Sorry you had to listen to all that. Sometimes I just need to talk...."

Uncle Darryl *does* come home safely, eight hours later. He is exhausted and stressed but completely okay otherwise. Aunt Debbie inquires about the woman—she made it to the hospital alive. You sleep better after that.

THE END

You leave the trees of the shoreline and follow the bleating sound up a rocky and grassy hill. The sight that greets your eyes is pitiful. A mother goat is pacing around a large, split rock. Wedged between the two rocks is a bleating baby goat. The mother runs away at your approach. You kneel down on the hot sun-baked surface of one of the rock halves and gently pull the baby goat out from between them. The goat kicks feebly. You set it on the ground. Walking on wobbly stilt-like legs, the baby goat tries to follow the direction that its mother took, only to faint with exhaustion. You could take the goat back home to Dave and Danielle's house to revive it. You could leave it there for its mother to find, but it would probably be dead by the time she comes back. Dave and Danielle might want it, or you could try to carry the baby goat back to its mother. The trouble is, she's afraid of you. What will you do?

(If you take the goat back to David and Danielle, go to page 169.)
(If you try to find the goat's mother, go to page 186.)

You close your fist around the worm, which is threatening to wriggle out into the canoe. Then you find the hook at the end of your line and carefully begin to thread the worm over it. Danielle already has a bite on her line. She pulls a shiny fish with large sharp fins into the boat. It is just slightly bigger than her hand. As you soon find out, their family rule states that you have to throw back any fish smaller than your hand size. She detaches the fish and lets it flop around in the bottom of the boat. "At least it will be dead soon," she says and hands her hook back to Dave to be re-baited. He had just finished baiting his hook.

You feel a small tug on your line. You pull a small, green silvery fish out of the water. It is only about three inches long, so you detach it from the hook and throw it back. A rumble of thunder fills the air as Dave opens the container to extract the next piece of worm.

"Oh, phooey," Danielle responds sadly, putting down her fishing pole and picking up her paddle.

"Yup," says Dave, putting down the margarine container and doing the same. "Well, at least we got *something* before the storm started." The three of you pull the boat all the way up onto shore and sit on the sides of it. The wind begins to blow hard, and the waves come crashing in, even more than before. It looks like you are going to witness a true Lake Victoria storm!

"We can't put the boat back out in the water," Danielle reasons. "Lightning."

"Can we drag it home?" you ask.

"I think that we should get Dad to drive the car over," Dave suggests. "We can carry the boat home on the roof rack of the car. I'll go get him," he announces, leaving you and Danielle sitting on the rim of the canoe.

As you sit there, you notice a group of women and girls peering at you and Danielle from around a clump of weeds. They giggle when you look their direction. You have a question for Danielle. "Is your family always this safety-conscious?"

"Well, yeah. I guess we're kind of extreme as missionary families go."

(If you are male, go to page 173.)
(If you are female, go to page 177.)

"Give me a foothold; like this." Dave locks his fingers together and holds them in a sling-like shape, palms up. You do the same. Dave plants one foot firmly into your hands and then puts all of his weight into it.

"Ouch!" you shout. Noise always helps sudden pain. You stagger but don't drop Dave's foot, though that is where the pain is coming from.

Dave plants his hands firmly, palms down, on the top surface of the rock and then pulls himself over the top. You pull two thorns out of your hands. The punctures have already begun to bleed. Maybe the thorns were only a quarter of an inch long, but Dave's weight managed to shove two of them to their full potential of harm.

"What happened?" Dave asks, peering over the edge of the rock.

"You had two stickers on the bottom of your shoe."

"Oh. Sorry. I guess I should have checked my shoes first." Dave stands up on the rock, slips, rights himself and then begins looking out. "I *still* can't see anything!" he laments. "But at least I can tell that we have drifted off course." He begins lowering himself down the side of the rock. You check the bottoms of his feet quickly before catching them just in time as his hands slip. You're not sure what happens next. You try to stabilize Dave, and it doesn't work. Soon he is rolling down the hill. You at least managed to slow his descent. What stops him is a tall green stalk with wimpy cabbage-like leaves at the very top. "Ahhhhh!" Dave cries out in pain. "I've hit an *mchicha* plant!" On closer examination of an identical plant near you, you discover the trunk to be coated with a fuzz of tiny, quarter-inch, needle-like thorns.

"What is going on?" Danielle appears from the bracken. Dave is ascending the hill, cradling one arm miserably.

"He rolled down the hill and hit an *mchicha* plant," you tell her. "I was helping him off the rock…he slipped…."

"I ran into an *mchicha* plant!" Dave calls out, moaning. From your angle, you can see that the shoulder of his tee shirt is stuck to him with small spikes.

"The poor *mchicha* plant. Now it can never fulfill its destiny as an edible vegetable. What's the problem, Dave?"

"Danny, I'm not talking about the little six-week-old spinach *mchicha* that we're forced to eat three times a week. I'm talking about a wild *mchicha* that has grown into a monster. It has just successfully avenged hundreds of its little brothers and sisters that I've consumed over the years. (I didn't like 'em anyway; *Mom* made me eat them.) This is unjust!"

"Dave, stop goofing! Do you think that you can take off your shirt?" Danielle asks.

"It's pinned to me in about one million places!" Dave cries in outrage. "Besides," he laughs weakly, "my tan is almost nonexistent!"

Danielle gives him a look.

"Oh, all right. Prepare to be blinded." Dave gingerly begins detaching the shirt from his shoulder and then, frustrated, rips it off with a yell.

"I think that got about half of them," Danielle reassures him.

"Yup," Dave grits his teeth. His lack of tan isn't nearly as bad as he made it out to be.

Danielle hands you his shirt. "Try to get the spines out of this; I'll work on Dave."

"If I can. These things are tiny!" You start working on it as Danielle goes to work on Dave with her fingernails, pulling out one spine at a time.

"So, Danny, how did you find us?" Dave is obviously trying to take his mind off the spines in his back. He jumps every couple of seconds.

"Well, I ran into a group of *kenges*, and then a black snake crossed my path," she says to you. "I ran away from it and then just happened to discover a thread of Dave's cargo shorts stuck on a bush."

"Right, Danny!" Dave says with sarcasm, then winces in pain.

"Read it and weep. See?" She hands him a khaki thread.

"Well done, Danielle Boone."

"And then I followed your trail and shoe prints through the bracken and found you here. There, I think I've gotten them all." Dave gets up and stretches.

"I think I've gotten them all out of your shirt too; no promises." You hand the shirt back to Dave, who gingerly puts it back on. "I don't know about you guys, but I've had enough of these islands for one day."

"I didn't know that *mchicha* plants could grow this big." Danielle is below, walking around Dave's adversary. "It was probably only defending itself."

"Yeah, right." Dave starts off.

"Goats!" Danielle calls out excitedly on the way back. Sure enough, up ahead are a billy goat and a nanny goat, enjoying the path that you and Dave blazed through the bushes. The going is quite a bit easier on the way back. You just follow your own trail. When you finally get under the shade of the mango tree, Danielle begins working on the combination lock, while Dave shoots mangoes with his slingshot. By the time you all actually pull away from the island, all of you have had a turn with the slingshot and there is a pile of dented, four-inch mangoes in the middle of the canoe.

When you get back home, Aunt Debbie makes you bleach the mangoes before eating them. You've never eaten anything so juicy or stringy. You could practically floss your teeth with them.

"Danielle, sick!" You look across the room to see Dave staring at Danielle in disbelief. "*You* should eat mangoes the African way." He takes his mango peel in his teeth, rips the peel off the mango and tosses it across the kitchen, narrowly missing the trash can. "Okay, so Africans don't eat mangoes indoors." He goes to pick up the peel from the floor.

"This is *also* an African way of eating a mango. It's neater!"

She bites into her mango, pulls off the peel with her teeth and then munches it happily.

Dave looks like he's going to choke.

"Dave, it's not like I'm eating a banana peel or something! Besides, mango peels from soft little mangoes taste good. You should try one."

Dave looks at the unpeeled side of his mango. "You have got to be kidding!"

For an answer, Danielle pulls the rest of the peel off her mango and stuffs it defiantly into her mouth.

Dave shrugs and takes a bite out of his mango peel. He spits it into the trash can, perfect aim this time. "There are some things that I will never understand about you, Danny."

She grins. Dave turns to you. "Okay, your turn. Come on, let's see you eat the peel."

"It's good!" Danielle affirms.

"Dare you," Dave smiles mischievously.

"Dave, they're not that bad!" Danielle chides him.

Will you? Or won't you?

THE END

"Climb a tree?" you half ask, half tell, Danielle, who has become rooted to the spot.

"Right!" Danielle jumps for a branch of a large tree nearby. Catching it with both hands, she holds the position of a "roasting pig" for one moment, before swinging herself on top of the branch and walking back along it to the trunk. You follow her and quickly discover that this isn't as easy as she made it look. It's still amazing what adrenaline can do. Once you are in the roasted-pig position, Danielle pulls you by your shirt; and soon you are lying on your stomach on top of the branch, hugging it for dear life. As you hold on, staring at the ground, one of the biggest pigs you've ever seen comes into view below. Ten little piglets follow it and then overtake it, heading in the direction of....

"Dave! " yells Danielle. "There's a whole herd of pigs coming your way!" You manage to sit up on your branch; then you follow Danielle higher into the tree.

She is trying to catch a glimpse of Dave from the tree-top. From your new perch you see Dave scamper up a skinny little tree. He's only about 7 feet off the ground, and you and Danielle are at least 20, so your view of him down below is perfect. The sow plops down under your tree, as if to make sure that you and Danielle leave her children in peace. The piglets keep running. They disappear under the trees below you for a moment and then reappear, playing, under Dave's tree.

"Ha! A 'whole herd of pigs,' huh?" Dave looks up to see you and Danielle in your tree, and he begins to roar with laughter. Danielle's shoulders droop in agitation. "You had me scared for a minute there!" Dave continues, "And to think that you two climbed all the way up there, to get away from…hmmha, ha, *ha!*" Dave dissolves into gales of laughter. He's laughing so hard that his spindly little tree shakes.

"No!" Danielle shouts, "There's a mother pig over here!"

Dave stops shaking for a moment. "Huh?"

"That's why we're scared!"

"Another? There's another? And that's why you guys are cowering up there!" He really loses it this time.

The sow is still plopped at the foot of your tree.

Danielle tries again. "We can't get down. There's a really big pig under our tree!"

"Oh, really? Only one? Well, let me see," he begins to count. "I've got ten. So, do you think mine could lick yours?"

You look down at the two-hundred-pound mama at the foot of your tree. "Not a chance."

"No way!" shouts Danielle.

"Sure they could! They've got tongues, haven't they?" At this Dave throws himself across a branch and howls.

Danielle turns to you. "He just doesn't get it. Dave," she shouts, "I'm serious!"

"If you two are going to sit up there, afraid of *one* pig," yells Dave, "I guess I'll just have to eat all these fruits myself!"

Dave has managed to lodge himself in a brush tree that has olive-like fruit. The fruit goes from green to white to purple, at which point they shrivel up and fall off the tree. They are slightly bigger than olives, have very large pits and taste bitter, Danielle explains. But when you're hungry....

"No!" You and Danielle watch, drooling, as Dave bites into one, obviously putting on more of a show than is necessary.

You and Danielle climbed up one of the biggest trees on the island. Looking out from it you can see almost the entire island. Birds have obviously had the same thought for centuries. This tree has no leaves and the tops of its branches are caked with white bird doo. The view is breathtaking, but that isn't what you are thinking about right now. Unable to get down, the two of you have realized that you are sitting in dry white paste, inches deep in some places.

"Please, Dave! The only thing edible in this tree is bird doo."

"What?" Dave yells back from his smaller tree, obviously enjoying himself thoroughly.

"Bird doo!"

"What about it?"

Danielle grabs a clump of bird doo off a nearby branch and pretends to eat it.

"Danny, you're sick!" yells Dave gleefully. She looks ready to throw some at him. He relents. "Okay, you guys, get into braced positions and I'll throw some fruit to you. But only after the meat course."

Dave shoots fruit at the piglets with his sling-shot. "Dave, you meanie!" shouts Danielle. He scares one piglet with a purposely misaimed shot and then begins to shoot the white-colored fruit to you. You now understand the importance of being in a braced position. It is quite tempting to throw yourself after all the stray missiles that just miss your hands. The branch in front of you prevents you from lunging too far from your center of gravity. Some of the fruits bounce off your tree and hit the mother pig below. She finally heaves her huge bulk up from under your tree and heads toward her piglets.

"She's coming!" Danielle shrieks excitedly to Dave.

"Yikes!" Dave gasps, dropping the fruit in his hand, which hits one of the piglets. At the approach of its mother, it begins to squeal more than is absolutely necessary.

The mother pig lets out an enraged yell and attacks the bottom of Dave's tree. Dave holds on tight as the tree begins to shake. Small fruits pelt down around her, making her more angry than ever.

"Yeeeeeeeeeeeeehhhhhhhhhhhhhaaaaaaaaaaaaaa hhhhhhhhhhhhhhhhhhhhh!" Dave yells, waving his baseball cap in the air as the tree jerks him every which way like a rodeo rider. He braces his legs in the branches, pulls out his ever-present slingshot, picks a small fruit out of a nearby cluster and aims. "Fire one!!!"

The mother squeals at this extra hard hit. The piglets have all run farther into the woods for safety. "FIEIEIIEIEIERE TTTTTTWOWOWOWO!!!!!" yells Dave as he is jerked violently from side to side. As the second fruit hits its mark, the mother pig oinks in defeat and runs off under the trees. Dave bows to you and Danielle, almost falling off his perch.

"Let's wait a while before we get down again." Danielle settles back against the trunk of the tree, oblivious to the white mess getting all over her clothes.

"Good idea," says Dave, who still looks shaken up.

"Well," Danielle calls to Dave, "after a snake and pigs, do you believe me now about the safety of these islands?"

"Give me a BB gun, some matches and my pocketknife," Dave sighs, "and I could survive out here for weeks."

A while later the three of you, all armed with tree sticks, climb down from your trees and race back to the canoe. You almost run over an unsuspecting monitor lizard in the process, which makes your flight even more exciting. Except for a few scrapes and scratches, you escape from the wild island of Isibinia unharmed. You have a lot to talk about at dinner that night, even if you didn't bring home the bacon.

The End

You and Danielle startle Dave by dashing around him, one on each side, and plunging ahead into the bracken through which he had been carefully weaving his way. "You guys!" he shouts after you, "is this a race or what?"

"Animals coming!" Danielle shouts back.

Dave glances quickly behind and then follows you, jogging easily through the cleared and broken path that you and Danielle create in your flight. He is just in time to see Danielle scream as a four-foot monitor lizard jumps off a nearby rock, landing right in front of her. You, running on Danielle's right, came very close to tripping over it as it lit off for the lake. It is amazing that any creature with legs that short could move so fast. It does have a very definite advantage in the vegetation that covers this side of Isibinia. The entire hillside seems to be overgrown with dry stick-type plants about four feet tall. Most of these sticks are covered in scratchy twigs and some have thorns.

A monitor lizard with its six-inch height can maneuver very easily through the lower trunks of these plants. A human being has more difficulty. These plants can scratch you raw, as you and Danielle just discovered.

You decide that now would be a good time to nurse your wounds. Danielle's lower shins are covered with scratches, and the hem of her skirt has a five-inch rip. She pulls up her socks to protect her shins for the remainder of the trip. Your arms are scratched, but no more harm has been done. Dave approaches nonchalantly, hands behind his back, whistling. "You know, you guys," he says, coming out of his reverie, "that was an excellent strategy! And I thought that the brush was going to beat us. But you two had the right idea! Full speed ahead! Blaze right through...."

"I'm glad you approve," Danielle interrupts him, "but we were running away from a herd of somethings."

Dave looks very close to laughter.

"I think that we need to head back to shore," Danielle says, looking at the blue lake far away. "We've wandered pretty far from it."

"Yeah," Dave agrees. Danielle begins to crawl away through the bracken, squeezing between the dry bushes. The smaller you can make yourself, the fewer the twigs you have to deal with. You notice ironically that she is following the same path that the escaping monitor took.

"Atta girl, Danielle! Going first!" Dave thanks his sister happily before crouching down on his haunches and following in her path. You follow Dave. Danielle turns suddenly and begins to follow a course perpendicular to the water. You find out why. The type of weed has changed. The bracken ahead has thorns. The dust flying up from the ground is mixing with your sweat, but you don't care. You had already tried to stand up once. It was like trying to put your head through a pile of firewood.

"I've made it!" You hear Danielle call from up ahead. At last you have left the bushes. What you have reached is a hillside of rocks. You all jump and slide down to the shoreline trees. Then you turn to your left and resume your original course.

You step between two trees and then stop, petrified. Dave and Danielle look as startled as you. If the island of Isibinia were the country of the monitor lizards, this stretch of rock beach ahead could easily be their capital city. The back of one lizard crawling into the woods directly ahead resembles a jagged tree trunk. You have counted ten monitor lizards, six you have seen, four you have definitely heard. The three of you quickly back up, tripping over each other in the process. You look back up the hill to the bracken and then consider your next course of action.

"I should have remembered that place from paddling." Dave grimaces.

Danielle agrees, "We always see *kenges* there when we go by in the boat. In fact, we saw two here earlier today, remember?"

"Well, we could just walk right through. We've seen how terrified these lizards are of us," Dave suggests. Danielle stares at him as if he's crazy.

"Scared of us? That crocodile back there did *not* look scared. He just walked off as though the sight of us repulsed his highness. I'm sure that if we waltzed right down Main Street and into his throne-room he'd have something else to say."

"That's true," Dave agrees grimly. "He went off exactly the way that we want to go. But maybe if we just give him enough warning, he'll clear out of his 'throne-room' as you call it before we pass right through."

He looks at Danielle's exasperated face. "Danielle, it's not that I *want* to go through Monitor City; it's just that I don't want to go back up the hill and battle the dry thorny brush again."

"I don't want to either," Danielle agrees, "but it is the only other option we have."

"You know, Danny, crawling through bracken isn't that much safer than walking through monitor territory. Monitor lizards run away, but if we found a snake up there in all that dry brush...."

Danielle shakes her head. "I just don't like huge lizards. Or snakes."

(If you would like to go back through the bracken, go to page 138.)
(If you would rather risk a stroll through Monitor City, go to page 142.)

You pick up the skull, hot to the touch from sitting out in the sun, and carry it back to the canoe. "It'll make a great souvenir," Dave says nobly.

You place it strategically in the front of the boat for your paddle home. The fishermen notice it on the way back. When you leave Tanzania, you have a rather impressive memento of your stay. It stinks up your suitcase on the way home, but who cares? It isn't everyone who can boast of having a monitor lizard skull!

THE END

Dave takes the monitor skull home and puts it in his room. To appease Danielle, he moves the cow skull out of his room and puts it on display in a tree in the front yard. In the end Aunt Debbie and Uncle Darryl don't like the image that this symbol of death gives to their visitors so Dave puts it over the front door of the smaller house (about six foot by eight foot) that he and his African friends are building in the yard. It goes beautifully with the rustic look of the building, which is made with poles and grass left over from the last time that the missionaries' grass roof was repaired. At last an arrangement was reached approved by all. Simba, the family dog, seems to take an uncanny interest in the little house after that.

THE END

"We're almost to the Shelf!" Dave says excitedly. You all just got out of the bracken and are walking through more navigable weeds.

"How do you know?" Danielle asks from behind you.

"How else? I've been up here before on one of our lunch trips. We're in Burrland!"

The tall sticklike growths all around you are covered in burrs at the top. "There it is!" Dave calls out, bursting out of Burrland and making his way down a steep, rocky, tree-shaded hill to the flat rock below sticking just out of the water. You know that it must be the bottomless cliff, and follow him down the hill around twisted trees. Peering over the side of the rock, you still can't tell how deep the water is; your reflection obscures all views. You and Dave look up in surprise as Danielle's reflection appears over the water. Her hair seems to have changed color. Looking directly at her, you see that her hair is completely

coated in burrs. She even has one stuck on her eyebrow. She looks at you and Dave and then glances up at her bangs, which are burr encrusted. She begins to slide the burrs out of her bangs with her fingers, one by one. "What I wouldn't give for a comb right now. It's at times like this that I wish I were a head taller!"

"Hail the burr queen!"

"Thank you, Dave." Danielle is still working the burrs out of her hair. "I wish we had brought some string to try to measure the depth of the water."

"We didn't think of it."

You follow in your own steps back across the island. Danielle ducks all the way back through Burrland but still comes out the crowned queen.

When you get to the canoe, you can't believe how exhausted you all are. You paddle home lazily under a beautiful sunset, glad that the water has calmed down. Pulling the canoe up the sandbank to the house is torturous. Uncle Darryl greets you at the door. "I guess you guys handled the storm all right. We wondered if we should go out and get you. I see that you did some exploring."

"How would you like a comb, Danielle?" Aunt Debbie offers.

Danielle's head began to itch on the way back, so of course she scratched it. Now her hair looks like a bird's nest. "I'd love one," Danielle says, almost sleepily. She wakes up immediately when her mother tries to comb the burrs out of her hair. They end up sliding the burrs out of her hair one by one.

The End

"Let's go through Monitor City," you suggest. "It will save time, and I don't think we're in any danger. Besides, you definitely don't want to crawl back through all that bracken!"

"I agree." Dave is retying his shoes.

Danielle has broken off a nearby little scrub tree at the trunk and is busy removing the branches. Dave looks at her questioningly. She explains, "I'm not going back through the bracken alone, and I'm not going through Monitor City unarmed." She keeps working at her rod.

"You know, Danielle, that's not a bad idea."

Soon all three of you are armed and ready to go through.

"This was your idea, so you guys go first." Danielle is unwilling to be the daring one.

"Fair enough." Soon you all venture out through the trees and onto the rocky beach, you and Dave at

the front and Danielle taking up the rear. The brush and trees practically reverberate with fleeing lizards.

"This might not be so bad after all!" says Dave on your right. He's watching a monitor swim away from shore. "Well, Main Street is over; here comes the courtroom."

"Try a 'bath house,'" Danielle comments over your shoulder.

Like parting a curtain, you and Dave push away the tree branches hanging down and peer into the "throne-room." What comes into view is a shady pool surrounded by large flat rocks on which more monitor lizards are lounging.

A searing pain cuts across your shins.

"You!!!" Dave screams at a monitor lizard below, swinging its tail, now bloody. It rallies for another offensive as Dave begins to beat it with his stick. You drop involuntarily on one knee, clutching the more painful of your two shins.

"We've got to get out of here, now!" Danielle grabs you by the arms and pulls you to a standing position while dragging you out. Once away from the throne-room door, she drops you and calls to Dave just as he bursts out of the leaves.

"They're coming!" he gasps. "Can you walk?" You try to rise to your feet as each takes one of your arms. You see blood smeared on your right hand and feel a renewed burning sting as you remove your hand from your left shin. Danielle and Dave pull you out of Monitor City and then stop partway up the rocky incline, still looking around nervously. You finally get to examine your shins. The front of your right shin is just barely cut through your blue jeans, but the front of your left shin, though hopefully not cut through to the bone, is gashed deeply. It is so full of blood that you can't tell much about it. If only you could have seen this result back when the three of you were standing in this very place, preparing to enter the Monitor City.

"We've got to stop that blood." Dave is getting ready to rip the bottom of his shirt.

"Dave, stop!" Danielle commands, ripping a strip of fabric off the bottom of her already torn skirt. "You've already lost a perfectly good pair of shoes; don't ruin your shirt. This skirt is already a rag."

"Shoes?" Dave asks, looking down at his feet.

"Look at the outer side of your right shoe," Danielle directs Dave. Then she turns to you. "I want to bandage up that gash."

"Ouch!" Dave exclaims as he sits down on a rock, clutching his ankle. He looks over at Danielle. "So I had a gash in my foot? Weird. It didn't hurt until you pointed it out."

Danielle has finished expertly tying up your leg and is now tearing a thinner strip from the bottom of her skirt. "You should be a nurse," you tell her.

"I know," she agrees. "I want to be one when I grow up."

"Hand over your foot," Danielle commands Dave, who is trying to take off his torn shoe and sock.

When he finally does, she begins to wrap the strip of fabric around it. "We'll have to get Mom to look at these when we get home. You guys might need stitches."

"Sorry about the smell of my feet," Dave says as Danielle leans close to them, tying the bandage just so.

"Funny," she says, sitting up again, "they didn't stink until you pointed it out."

"Oh, be quiet," Dave grunts.

The trail is easier going back, now that it has been cleared of bracken. But the going is slower. Danielle is the only one still able to crouch on both feet. Though shorter, her skirt still falls well below her knees. She says she'll just hem it up when you all get home.

Paddling back home is also a slower process. The waters have calmed down, but you never realized that paddling involved your shin muscles. Danielle and Dave assure you that you don't have to paddle, so you don't. You and Dave don't have to drag the canoe either when you get home. Uncle Darryl and Danielle do it. When you get up to the house, Aunt Debbie examines both of you. She numbs the area of the gashes and gives you and Dave stitches. It looks like you and Dave won't be going anywhere for a while. Both of you have to admit that Danielle was right in her fear of monitor lizards, though you think that it is decent of her not to flaunt it over you.

THE END

Danielle is smiling happily as you all make your way around on the shoreline, under dark, overhanging trees. The shoreline is steep, so you move carefully from jutting rock to rock, holding onto roots and weeds to keep from sliding down the bank.

With the next cove comes a revolting smell. Noticing the silvery object dashing against the rocks, you gather that the storm has washed in a rotten fish. You have no way to pinch your nose; you need both hands to keep from sliding into the water. You get away from there as quickly as you can.

Danielle suddenly gets excited. She runs ahead, slipping and sliding, to where a large tree has fallen down over the water. She walks out on its rough trunk, looking down at the waves beneath her. Making it to the upper branches of the tree, she sits down comfortably and looks toward the point on the mainland. "I can see our rock from here!"

"That's great," Dave acknowledges. "I'm going to it!"

He heads off, once again along the shoreline. Danielle sighs, gets off the tree and follows. As you approach a flat rocky beach, two brown monitor lizards scurry off, one up the shore and one into the water. When you finally reach the rock, you find out that it's too far out in the water to get to without getting wet. You can experience the storm very well from the beach. The lake stretches to the horizon. Lightning slices the distant sky, and the waves are battering furiously against the rocks. The storm is truly majestic. "Oh, by the way!" Danielle informs you, shouting against the wind. "There is a sailboat out that way somewhere," she points off to the left. "It's actually a really nice one, without very many rips in the sail. I think it was a charcoal carrying ship."

"Those are usually loaded to within a couple of inches from the waterline!" Dave adds, shocked. "It was out in this weather?"

"That's right," Danielle affirms.

"Wait, I think I see it!" Dave points. You squint in the direction that he's pointing. There's some kind of ship there, but it doesn't have a sail. Unless....

"It tipped over!" Danielle says frantically.

Dave is thinking aloud. "This island is blocking it from the view of the mainland, so no one there will be able to see the sailboat. We can barely see it! Then, of course, there's the bad weather. Most other boats would have gone inland by now. Most Africans here can't swim...."

"Can't *swim?*" you interrupt. "They live by Lake Victoria!"

"They don't know how to swim," Dave restates. "They don't usually use life jackets or emergency flotation devices either. That leaves this up to us!"

Danielle feels that an explanation of the swimming issue is in order. "Probably no one has ever known how to swim, so no one has ever taught anyone else. People *are* afraid of drowning, for understandable reasons."

"Let's get going!" Dave calls out.

"Wait, Dave!" Danielle skids along the steep shoreline after him, climbing over large rocks. "You aren't thinking about taking the canoe out there to rescue four or five men in *this* weather, are you? The boat will be swamped!"

"No, I'm not," he answers. "What we have to do is hope that the boat stays afloat out there long enough for us to get home and get Mom and Dad. They can take out the motorboat."

When you all reach the canoe, Dave quickly unchains it and you all pile in. You forget your life jackets and have to paddle back to shore to get them. You decide to paddle out back through the channel and around the other side of Isibinia. It's a longer distance, but at least the waves are blocked on that side of the island.

No one talks on the strenuous trip home. When you finally make it back, you tell Uncle Darryl and Aunt Debbie about the sailboat. They waste no time. Uncle Darryl grabs extra life jackets and Aunt Debbie grabs blankets and her medical kit.

Through the rest of the day you watch the operation unfold. Uncle Darryl and Aunt Debbie bring back the people from the boat, who then begin organizing the other boats down by the market into a recovery squad to tow the partially submerged sailboat into land. Many little canoes paddle out to the sailboat to rescue the soaked charcoal. Later in the evening when the water calms, the sailboat is finally towed into shore.

The End

"You guys!" They turn to look at you. "I've picked up some kind of rash."

Danielle climbs back down the hill.

"Is it bad?" Dave calls down to you.

"I need to borrow your tweezers, Dave." Danielle goes into action.

"That bad, huh?" Dave climbs back down the hill and pulls a Swiss Army Knife out of his pocket. "Uh, oh. I guess the tweezers are missing out of this knife. I still have the toothpick, though!" He pulls it out proudly.

"Oh, yeah, that'll help a lot, Dave." Danielle studies the back of your hand, takes one of the hairs between the ends of her finger and thumbnail, and then jerks it out.

"Yeowch!" That really hurt.

She's about to pull the next one. Your hand jerks violently, expecting another sharp pain. "Why don't you sit down?" Danielle motions you to a nearby rock.

Dave looks at your hand. "That has all the marks of a furry caterpillar."

Danielle jerks out another hair and holds it up to the light. You glimpse barbs on the ends. "Once I get all of these hairs out, we'll have to go home and put some cortisone cream on the rest of it. Don't scratch, whatever you do. The infection can spread."

"I already did scratch," you admit.

"Oh, well; how could anyone help scratch a furry caterpillar rash?"

"Whatever you do, don't rub your eyes," says Dave, peering over Danielle's shoulder as she reaches for another hair.

"Wait a minute! That's one of *my* hairs!" You don't want to go through any more pain than is absolutely necessary.

"Sorry." Danielle lets go of it and goes for another caterpillar hair. Your hand does feel better once all of the caterpillar hairs are out. You grip your paddle tightly as you paddle home, trying to keep yourself from scratching. It's hard. The cortisone cream is a welcome relief once you get back to Dave and Danielle's house.

Danielle comes to get you. "An elder of the church just arrived; we need to go and greet him." You, Dave and Danielle greet the man out in the family living room. He seems very old and walks with a cane, but he's glad to see you. Uncle Darryl comes out with a card and gives it to the man, speaking in Kiswahili and pointing to various sizes of type on the card.

"He's come to get reading glasses," Dave explains. "In our home country there's an eye doctor who mails us pairs of simple reading glasses to give away here."

"2.75," Uncle Darryl says to Danielle. She goes into their parents' bedroom to find the right sized pair.

"Ministries come in all shapes and sizes," Dave comments. "It really does a lot for a church when the elders are able to read the Bible on their own."

THE END

"I would rather go to the caves," you tell them.

"Okay," Dave agrees. "I'll bet if we head across the island that way," he points inland and a bit to the left, "we'll end up right on top of the caves. Let's go." You start off through the trees. Soon you reach a steep hillside. It is a mixture of vines, rocks, grass and bracken. You all climb it on all fours to keep from slipping. When you reach the top, you dust off your hands and look around. You can see the lake on three sides and most of the island.

"I'm about ready to give up this whole cave quest just to explore this place," Dave sighs, "but first things first. If we head down this hill on our left, and then climb that hill over there, we'll make it."

This is easier *said* than done. The hill that you descend next is covered in thorns and sticker bushes.

"Could you help me a minute?" Danielle asks from behind you. You see that her hair is caught in a branch full of short thorns. "I can't untangle it because I can't see it!" You begin the painstaking process of unwinding her hair from the thorn branch, while Dave hikes back up the hill towards you.

He begins helping. "How do you manage it, Danny? Ow!" he exclaims, discovering a thorn hidden in the tresses.

"I actually have hair," she explains shortly.

"My hair isn't that short!" Dave defends himself.

"But it doesn't get caught in trees," Danielle argues, as the last strand of her hair comes free.

"You should try wearing hats!" Dave plops his hat down on Danielle's head and stomps off down the hill.

"This might actually help!" Danielle puts it on backwards. The quarrel seems resolved after that. As you finish sliding down the last part of the incline, you realize that somewhere in all of this crawling around, you picked up a rash on the back of your left hand, especially in the area between your thumb and forefinger. Danielle and Dave are already climbing the hill in front of you. The rash itches like crazy. You scratch it, only to receive sharp pains, as though your hand were stuck with pins. You can actually see various points that look like hairs speckled across the rash. If you touch it, it burns; if you leave it alone, it itches terribly, but you might be able to ignore it and keep going.

(If you go down to the lake and wash immediately, go to page 66.)
(If you ask Dave and Danielle what you should do about it, go to page 152.)
(If you ignore it and keep going, go to page 158.)

You're not going to let a rash ruin your day, even if it is a bad one. Climbing the next steep hill turns out to be another four-footed operation. You accomplish it as best you can with only three: two feet and one hand. Disentangling the back of your shirt from a thorn bush proves an especially difficult task. At last you make it to the top of the hill. Danielle and Dave are already scurrying down the other side of the hill. The hill is steep and covered in boulders. The rain has washed around them to form many small caves underneath. Danielle and Dave are staring into a cave just below when several small hand-sized bats fly out. Just then a large monitor lizard crawls out of one of the caves below them and splashes into the water.

"So do you still want to go in there?" Dave asks Danielle as you approach.

"Not really." Danielle notices you. "Do *you* want to try to go in there? Any *kenges* would have left by now, and I'm sure that we've scared most of the bats away."

"Danielle, are you planning to use our guest for a guinea pig?"

"Certainly!" Danielle turns pleading eyes to you, "Please? Will you do it? Go into the cave?"

"I've seen enough of the caves," Dave interjects. "It's four o'clock, and we have to start back by five. If we leave now and start heading back to the canoe, we'll be able to explore more of the island. Or, if you guys want, we could hang out longer at these caves. I don't really care but...."

(If you would like to go into the cave, go to page 160.)
(If you would rather explore more of the island on your way back, go to page 193.)

Why not go in? Who's afraid of a few bats? You stick your head into the mouth of the cave. The smell of bat guano is stifling, but you are determined to go through with this. You walk to the back of the cave and then turn to face Dave and Danielle. Danielle immediately follows you, holding her nose. Dave says that he can't stand the smell. You believe him too. It's time to get out for a breath of fresh air.

"Kiss…me," says Danielle.

"What?" you ask, startled.

"Huh?" Dave peers into the cave.

"Look up there! It's written on the wall!" Danielle is pointing upwards at the rock wall of the cave.

"Kiss me," you read. There are two words written on the wall in white capital letters.

"Writing on the wall?" This is enough to bring even Dave into the smell. He looks at it, laughs,

coughs and leaves. You and Danielle are ready to get out of there too.

"Probably some secondary school student wrote that," Danielle decides.

"And to think," Dave sighs dejectedly, "that I thought that it was going to be a note from Henry Stanley. We could have been famous! 'I, Henry Stanley, stood in this cave in 1875....'"

"Dave, how did you remember that!"

"Don't you remember? Last year we studied great explorers, and Mom gave us a test that included the dates of their explorations."

"Well," Danielle shrugs, "I probably learned the dates for the test and then forgot them. I don't even remember all the names of the U.S. presidents that I memorized last year."

"The only one that I remember is James A. Garfield. And George Washington, of course."

"I sometimes wonder if home schooling is more difficult than other types of schooling." Danielle sits down.

"It depends on who your teacher is," Dave tells you. "Our mom is a good one, though. She doesn't push us ahead (though I'm a grade ahead in math and Danielle reads two grades ahead; we're good at those subjects). We do well on achievement tests."

"Except for that one test where I had to explain how to use a phone book. As you know, we don't have a phone; only a radio."

"I wonder how secondary students got out here to the island?" Dave muses, sitting down as well. "So how do you know that the secondary school students are the ones who wrote 'KISS ME' on the wall? Maybe Henry Stanley was feeling amorous."

Danielle gives him a look and then begins to explain. "A while back we went to the graduation ceremony of the secondary school. The students did traditional dancing, a magic show, an acrobatic show and other things."

"Yeah, but not kissing," Dave clarifies.

"Well," Danielle continues, "some of the speeches given by various men were boring, so I was looking around. Every single chair in the Kahunda Secondary School has KSS written on the back in white paint to identify it. On one of the chairs, some-one had filled in an 'I' with a black pen between the 'K' and the 'S', and, well, you can guess the rest. The left side of your face is all red," Danielle tells you suddenly.

"So is your neck," Dave says from behind you.

You realize that your face and neck have started to itch, just like your hand. This is no time to beat about the bush. "A while back this rash started on my left hand, and I must have rubbed it on my face and neck. It's like I have these tiny splinters in my hand that won't come out...."

"Let me see it." You hold out your left hand to Danielle. She takes your hand gingerly, avoiding the red patches. As soon as she sees the "splinter," she is convinced. "It was a fuzzy caterpillar, and you've spread the rash around. Sorry. I mean, it's hard not to scratch. Those things itch a lot...." Danielle jerks on the hair with her fingernails and one of them comes out. Needless to say, your hand feels a bit better. She starts pulling more.

"It's time to go," Dave cuts in.

You feel better after you've gotten back to the house, taken a shower and put cortisone cream on all of the rash; but it is still hard to sleep that night.

THE END

"Ready!" You raise your paddle. There isn't a moment to lose; are you going exploring or not?

"That's the spirit!" Dave is excited.

You make a beeline for the beach of Isibinia. Keeping an eye out for anything moving, another snake perhaps, you jump out of the canoe as it scrapes on shore. The stability of land feels strange. Danielle gets out, glancing carefully around for predators as she takes off her life jacket. Dave steps out of the boat with the lock and chain, drags the canoe farther up the beach and then begins to padlock it to a small tree.

"You were planning for this all along, weren't you?" Danielle asks.

"Yup," Dave answers, intent on his work. He steps back. "You know, if someone wanted to steal our boat, they could easily break this tree in half. We need to find a bigger tree. Come on, you guys, let's drag the boat inland!"

"Here we go." You, Danielle and Dave drag the boat into the nearby path which opens up between tall flower bushes. You turn a corner through your passageway and arrive in a small clearing with a large tree growing in the middle of it.

"A mango tree!" You all hang your life jackets behind one particularly thick bush, where they won't be seen.

"Not a movie wilderness, huh, Danielle?" Dave asks. "Here's a tree full of fresh fruit!"

"Dave, I didn't want to get off on these islands in the first place, so couldn't you at least try to be nice while we're here?"

"Sorry." Dave chains the canoe to the mango tree and sighs with satisfaction. "Now that we don't need to worry about the boat, we can go anywhere! We might as well start down that path. I hope this island isn't completely overrun by paths; it's more fun to explore off the beaten track. You don't have to come, Danny."

"I would rather not be left alone. Let's go." Danielle sets off determinedly down the path. Dave follows her. You follow Dave. There is a loud rustling in the bushes off to the right, going away from you. That was no small creature. You're beginning to wonder if this was such a good idea. Dave seems to be having the same thoughts. Danielle seems to consider the noise as just part and parcel of going on a dangerous venture like this. You come out into a dry field. A way off, a hill rises in front of you. Behind, trees cut off your view of the lakeshore.

"So where are we going?" Danielle asks. "This is your expedition, Dave."

"The caves, of course. Where else?"

"Well," Danielle comments thoughtfully, "we could go there. Or we could try to go to our normal picnic spot. It's also on the other side of the islands, just more to the right."

"Normal picnic spot? Oh, you mean the Shelf," Dave clarifies.

"The Shelf, the Bottomless Cliff. Whatever you want to call it."

"I appoint our guest the official decision maker. Where should we go?"

"So what exactly is the Bottomless Cliff?" you ask.

Danielle tells you. "On the other side of the island, there is a shelf of rock sticking just above the water that we like to drag our canoe on when we go to the island to eat lunch. Well, one day Dave brought an anchor and dropped it over the edge of the shelf to try to anchor the boat. What we didn't know was that the shelf is actually a vertical rock that drops at least 40 feet down into the water. That was as far down as our anchor rope would go. It would be a great diving rock, if we were allowed to touch the lake water."

"So which place will it be?" Dave asks. "Both of those places are really far away, so we need to get started soon. If we go to the Shelf, we should follow the shoreline. There will be fewer brambles that way, and we'll be sure to get where we are headed. If we go to the caves, it would make sense to cross the island directly, seeing that the caves are about as opposite to where we are as they could be. I promise you," Dave says to you, "make this one last decision for us, and then we'll get started."

(If you want to try to cross the island to get to the caves, go to page 87.)
(If you want to try to cross the island to get to the caves, go to page 87.)
(If you want to try to follow the waterline to get to the Shelf, go to page 95.)

You follow your steps back to the lakeshore, and from there, back out to the valley. You climb the last hill where David and Danielle were, hoping that they didn't go much farther. They must not have because you can hear their voices. At the top of the hill you stand looking down over a rocky cliff that slopes steeply down to the lake. From the sounds of their voices Dave and Danielle must be inside the hill, obviously in a cave. Dave walks out of one of the caves and begins scraping his shoes on a nearby ridged rock. "Goat housekeeping," he mutters.

"Maaaaa!" says the little goat, reviving for a moment in your arms, probably from the familiar smell. Dave stops dead with his back to you and then slowly turns around.

"Oh, hi," he says, seeing you, and then squints at the little goat. "What in the...."

"Dave," says Danielle, coming out of the cave, "speaking of goats, I think I just heard...." and then she sees you. "Oh, my word! Where did you find it?"

"Danny, the animal lover," Dave sighs.

"I found it stuck in a split rock," you tell her.

Danielle is now balancing precariously beside you on a rock, looking at it. "What a *little* guy, still in his clumsy stage. Where's your mother?" she croons.

"She ran off when I found him," you explain quickly.

"Well, we need to take this liddle guy home and give him some milk. He's nearly dead!"

"Danny, Mom and Dad don't want a goat. It will eat every plant in the yard! We need to find the mother."

"We can try," Danielle agrees, "but if we don't find his mother in time, we're taking him home. We can bring him back here once he gets better."

Dave may have called Danielle the "animal lover," but from the look in his eyes you know that there must be some of it in him too.

"We can't really leave it to *die*...." he begins.

"Right," Danielle says quickly. "Let's go."

"Why don't we give it some water first?" Dave suggests.

"Can it drink *water*?" Danielle asks.

"That's the main component in milk, isn't it? Here, give it to me." Dave makes his way down to the lake and scoops water for the goat in a leaf. Then he comes back up the hill. "We should at least try to look for the mother, but he's really bad off. Maybe we *should* take him back home."

Danielle winks at you. "We could just leave him in the goat cave. That's his home, isn't it?"

"No, I meant home with his mother, or with us if that's the way it ends up. Let's go."

You all take turns carrying the baby goat as you return to the spot where the mother goat ran off. For a while you are able to follow her tracks, but then it is obvious that she must have taken to mountain-goating. Her tracks in the dirt stop immediately before a rocky hillside. In the end you are unable to find her.

You get home as quickly as you can. Uncle Darryl and Aunt Debbie are both surprised at the arrival of Herbert, as he becomes called, and agree that sooner or later he'll have to be returned to the islands. Within a day, Herbert is moved out of the house and into the yard. Within two days, Herbert is following everyone around. He seems confused as to who is his mother and follows whoever brought him food more recently.

It soon becomes apparent that Herbert is ready to return to the islands; he's beginning to eat greens and doesn't need food brought to him any more.

You go with Dave and Uncle Darryl to the island.

As soon as Herbert begins to "Maaaaa!," the mother goat appears. You witness a happy reunion. She knew her baby's voice immediately.

It's time for you to return to your country. You forget about washing your hands in the lake until you are tested and treated for bilharzia six months later. Unfortunately, a quick solution created a more long-term problem.

THE END

A crowd continues to gather as you wait for Dave to come back. When Danielle takes off her bright orange life jacket, the crowd roars with laughter. "What's the big deal?" asks Danielle, in English. "I'm not stripping!"

As more people arrive, the old-timers, or all of those who saw Danielle's performance, describe through hand motions what it looked like when Danielle took off her life jacket. You decide to take off yours, just for the show value. The crowd loves it. Just when you are expecting them to call for an encore, the truck drives up. The people watch in silence as the four of you raise the canoe onto the roof. You are relieved when you all finally drive away from the mass of eyes and back to the missionaries' yard.

THE END

About a quarter of a mile down the beach is a triangular peninsula of sand that juts out from the land and shields the bay from the open part of the lake. (The second largest lake in the world can be very wavy.) Out on this point are several groups of fishermen, pulling in nets. The nets are shaped like mesh hammocks with extra long ropes. They are each made up of a pocket-shaped net, about 12 feet wide, with a long rope attached to each side. The fishermen put the net and rope in a wooden canoe, and then after leaving one rope end in the hands of a person on shore, they paddle in a wide arc out into the lake, lowering the rope and net over the side of the canoe as they go. When the canoe arrives back at the shore a few feet from the place where it started, the real work begins. The two rope ends are pulled by groups of men until the net arrives on shore with all of the unlucky fish that happened to be in its path.

As you walk out onto the point, you are struck with a serious case of squinting. You try to shade your eyes, but the light mirrored off the waves and sand is still blinding. As soon as the fishermen notice Dave, you begin to hear cries of *"Bwana Samaki!"* You find out that this is the fishermen's name for Dave, and its meaning is none other than "Mr. Fish." A dancing young man approaches, delighted to see all of you. He is happily jumping and bouncing around to the sound of a faraway radio. As Dave heads across "the point" to a net way off on the other side of the one that just came in, you begin to wonder about the odd, dancing man following you. Dave and Danielle explain to you that they are quite familiar with this man. So familiar, in fact, that *they* have christened him with his own name, none other than "Mr. Dance." He's quite harmless, they assure you. You can't help but notice how closely Danielle sticks by Dave.

The fishermen are busy pulling fish out of the net by the gills and then slinging them into the sand. Dave, an expert in his trade, judges that two of the fish would be just right for a meal for you all. A hard bargaining session and 800 Tanzanian shillings later (about one American dollar), you are on your way home.

(Go to page 189.)

A group of three fishermen are heading in your direction. They are young, probably in their late teens or early twenties. The giggling women and girls behind you have disappeared. "Hurry, Dave!" Danielle moans. "Sometimes these fishermen aren't very polite, and I don't like the looks on their faces." The men are laughing, but as they approach you see the malicious, uncurbed look in their eyes and understand Danielle's uneasiness.

"*Hallo!*" says one in a forced high squeaky voice. "*Una fanya nini?*"

"*Ninasubiri baba yangu,*" she replies tensely.

They begin to imitate her Kiswahili once again in high squeaky voices.

"What happened?" you ask.

"They asked me what I was doing, and I told them that I was waiting for my dad. They probably think I'm just trying to scare them away. Ignore them if you can."

One walks over, picks up one of the fishing poles and begins to play with the reel. "*Acha!*" Danielle commands angrily.

"*Acha! Acha!*" they imitate once again in high squeaky voices, as the other two men each pick up a fishing pole.

"You're gonna tangle it!" Danielle cries out in English. It probably wouldn't have done any more good if she had said it in Kiswahili. Sure enough, one of the reels is already tangled. The man turns the handle every which way, trying to figure out how it works. Danielle tries to take it from his hand, but he holds it out of her reach, laughing. She comes back and sits down. "He knows I can't stop him. If I tried, he and his buddies might have to teach me my place in society." The second of the reels is already stuck because of tangles. The third man hasn't tangled the one he picked up. He has loosed the catch and is pulling skeins of fishline into a tangled mass on the grass.

"He says he can't understand why white people need to carry such a long line on their poles," Danielle relates bitterly. "He says that maybe we always *break* our lines."

One of the other men has figured out the system. The other two gather excitedly behind him for a demonstration. You hear the sound of a truck in the distance. The young men begin to glance at each other nervously.

"*Ni baba yangu!*" Danielle proclaims triumphantly. The men begin to back away. When they see the car round the bend, they run off to a safe distance of about 60 yards. The red pickup truck with a cap over the back pulls up. Dave and Uncle Darryl get out. Simba, who ran alongside the car all the way, runs up and begins to lick Danielle's face where frustrated tears were forming. She puts her arms around the dog's neck. "Yes, Simba. I love you too. And I wish you had been here just a little while ago."

You notice that the three fishermen retreat even farther away as soon as Uncle Darryl and Dave get out of the car. They move even farther away when Uncle Darryl and Dave spot the fishing poles.

"Danny, what happened to these reels?" Dave picks them up furiously.

"Those men over there were 'playing' with them," Danielle points to the three fishermen.

"Well? Didn't you tell them to stop? To '*acha*'?" Dave asks.

Danielle can't stand it any longer. She explodes. "Of course I told them to '*acha*'! You know very well that men in this culture don't obey girls. They can pick on us all they want, and nobody cares! But if you or you, Dad," she says to her father, "raised your finger to them, they'd stop whatever they were doing!"

"Not all young men here pick on you!" Dave protests. "Some fishermen have a bad reputation, but you can't make it sound like everyone is that way!"

Uncle Darryl is looking at the reels. "Well, Dave," he says to his son, "I'm going to go have a little 'talk' with those men who picked on your sister and friend. Would you like to join me?"

"With pleasure!" says Dave, cracking his knuckles appreciatively. Simba wags her tail excitedly. The three of them start off in the direction of the three men. You never saw anyone run so fast. Danielle was right; they were cowards. Uncle Darryl and Dave come right back to load the boat onto the truck as soon as they see that the men clearly aren't interested in "talking," but Simba, seeing them run, chases them out of sight, barking authoritatively. Then she comes back.

"Sorry, you guys," says Dave. "I shouldn't have left you two here by yourselves this close to the fishing grounds."

You all lash the canoe onto the top of the car and drive home. "I'm sorry that you had to experience that," Danielle says to you on the way back home in the car. "But in a way, I'm glad that it happened. Now you know what I go through. It's one of the worst things about living out here, and it never happens when the men in my family are with me."

THE END

"Why don't we just wait out the storm?" you suggest. "We don't want to chance lightning, and this island isn't exactly a petting zoo! Let's just sit here on the beach until the storm quiets down. If anything else shows up, our boat will be right within reach!"

Dave and Danielle have to admit that you have the best idea. Dave is still disappointed. "So what are we going to do now?"

"Play tic-tac-toe in the sand, I guess," Danielle suggests as you pull the canoe onto the beach. For a while, life is fairly interesting. Every once in a while fishes will leap completely out of the water in the channel. One is over a foot long. They aren't easy to spot; they jump quickly, so you have to be looking in exactly the right place at exactly the right time. There's no telling when or where one will jump next, and you never hear a splash until they reenter the water.

Just then you see something else pop out of the water. Some animal out in the channel just poked its head up to look at you. "You guys!" you call Dave and Danielle. The animal goes back underwater.

"What?" Dave comes over.

"I saw an otter!" Danielle calls from the other side of the beach. Sure enough, at least three otters in the channel seem to be as interested in you as you are in them. Dave congratulates you for spotting the first mammal. After a while, he gets bored watching the water and starts gazing more frequently at the path leading away from the beach. "You guys, I think that's a mango tree just inland. I want to go check it out."

"Well, I'm not going," Danielle announces. You and she have resorted to a game of tic-tac-toe in the sand.

"I'm going," Dave trudges off down the path.

After a while you and Danielle give up tic-tac-toe. Danielle has offered to teach you an African game called Bao. She digs a set of holes in the sand, four holes wide and nine holes long. Now you and she are searching for the required number of pebbles with which to play.

That's when Dave comes dashing back down the path. "Into the boat, now!" His face is pale.

"What?" Danielle drops her pebbles.

"No questions! Into the boat!" After the snake incident earlier, you and Danielle know better than to argue.

Once you're out in the channel, Danielle reassures you, "We have an actual Bao game at home. It's carved out of wood, with real round seeds to play with. I can teach you there."

"You mean to tell me that you guys aren't even interested in why we had to leave the island so fast?"

"Well, okay. Why?" Danielle picks up her paddle demurely. The storm has quieted down, and you haven't heard thunder for a while.

"Because down that path is the biggest pig you ever laid eyes on!"

Danielle giggles.

"You don't believe me?" Dave is affronted.

"No, I believe you. We've seen pigs on the shore before."

"Believe me, they seem a lot bigger when you're as close to one as I was!"

After a strenuous paddle, you pull the canoe up on the beach. You did hear two more peals of thunder, but God protected you on the way home. You drag the boat up the sandy hill in a series of short bursts. Once you're on level ground in the yard, the going gets easier. You all have to step carefully over and around a very affectionate black cat who is trying to rub against all of your legs. "Don't be fooled by her affectionate facade," Dave warns. "It's her dinnertime."

"It's ours too," Aunt Debbie comments, coming out onto the back cement-slab porch. "Dave, please go down and get a couple of fish from the fisherman. I'm running late on dinner today, and fish is so quick and easy!"

"After I do all the work, of course," Dave grins.

"Of course!" Aunt Debbie walks back into the house with Dave to get some money.

"Mom doesn't like fish," Danielle tells you, after her mother reenters the house. "But even she would admit that the freshwater fish we get here by the lake are the best you can get anywhere."

Dave comes out with a plastic bag and a couple of Tanzanian bills.

"Do you guys want to come along?" he asks.

"I think I'll go," Danielle decides.

(If you would like to get fish with Dave and Danielle, go to page 174.)
(If you would rather stay home until they get back, go to page 189.)

The goat tracks lead right into the impressive island bracken. Since you picked up the little goat, you have received two fleabites. You just hope that this business will be over quickly. You put the goat into a football hold under one arm and use the other to push twiggy branches out of your face. You glimpse the mother goat up ahead and sigh with relief, thinking that the chase is ended; but she runs away from you. If you could only get the little goat some water, then it might revive, and you could leave it, bleating in a place where its mother could find it. You don't want to lose the trail of the mother goat, though, so you continue to follow it. She seems to be heading for the lake anyway (but any straight path across an island always winds up at the lake).

When the lake finally comes into view, you see the mother goat drinking water down the shore. She was thirsty too. You sneak down to the lake, dip your fingers into the water, and then wet the muzzle of the

baby goat. It gasps. You dip the edge of your T-shirt into the water and give it to the goat to suck on. The goat drinks. Finally it begins to revive. The mother goat is still in sight. You place the goat, crying pitifully, on the ground and begin to back away. It follows you.

"No, not me! Go to your mother." It is still trying to follow you. And then....

"Maaaaa?" calls the mother goat.

"Maamaa!" calls the little goat and runs off in the right direction. The reuniting of mother and baby is sweet but not sappy. The nanny goat begins to lick her baby as it nurses hungrily. Then she gives you a disgusted look before walking away, her little goat following happily in tow. She obviously wasn't happy to find your smell on her little goat, even though you were the one who saved its life.

The trouble now will be explaining to Dave and Danielle where you were all this time and finding out, by test or by time, whether or not you got bilharzia.

THE END

Dave and Danielle's first order of business when they return from getting fish is to greet a visitor who arrived at the house. Both shake her hand while she sits on the couch. They say, "*Shikamo.*" Danielle does a curtsey with her greeting. You find out that all girls and women are required to curtsey at the start of any interaction with someone older than they are. "I have one very strong knee now from greeting people," Danielle explains, as she easily demonstrates the deep up and down kneeling motion that she completes several times on a daily basis. "At church I greet at least 50 people every Sunday, one curtsey after another, and at big social events, like Easter services, I greet more! That can get really tiring after a while."

Dave puts the narrower and still-living fish into a bucket of water to keep it fresh while he begins to clean the dead one. He finishes scaling it, and then removes the head, the backbone, the tail, all the fins and the entire digestive tract. Danielle comes out onto the porch to where you and Dave are standing, carrying the sloshing red bucket with the other fishes in it. Dave looks up from his wooden cutting board, scaling knife in hand. "Uh, oh. I've seen this before—Danny with our living dinner. Bad combination. I shouldn't have left the fish in the house...."

"Dave, we need a fishpond!" she announces happily.

Dave nods at you. He shrugs, motions out to Lake Victoria and then goes back to cleaning the fish. "I think that counts, doesn't it?"

"No, we need a small one in the yard. We could put live fish into it and have fresh fish at any time! Besides, they would be fun to watch and to feed. We could make it with a piece of plastic or cement, if we wanted to go for the elaborate!"

"The cat would love it," Dave replies, not looking up.

You hear the sound of a piteous mewing coming from the locked storeroom nearby. Dave obviously didn't appreciate the "help" of the cat with his fish gutting.

"I still think it would be a good idea," Danielle says with a pout. "We'll have enough fish to spare. Besides, Chiro is a very normal cat who doesn't like to get wet."

"And what about Simba?" Dave asks, motioning with his head toward the hound chained by the collar to a tree a short distance away. With a wrinkled brow and half-raised ears, the Rhodesian Ridgeback looks absolutely pathetic. Dave didn't appreciate her "help" either.

"Simba would try to catch the fish and then choke on the fish bones," Dave argues.

"True," Danielle agrees. "But maybe if we only put little pet fishes in the pond." She looks sadly at the bigger fish in the bucket and then brightens. "Like those!" she exclaims in astonishment and delight. You go over and look too. A dozen little inch-long fishes are swimming around in the bucket water. Dave comes over and peers down, knife in hand.

"Okay, Danny, where did you get them?"

"I didn't!" she exclaims happily.

"Maybe there were fish in the water that I put into that bucket," Dave thinks to himself.

"Dave, all of our water comes from a well!" Danielle giggles.

"Are you implying that that fish managed to lay eggs in the bucket in the last hour and they have hatched?" Dave scratches his head.

"I'm not implying anything, Dave," Danielle protests. "The evidence is there!" You agree. Those little fishes are certainly alive, and from Dave's complete willingness to believe that Danielle didn't put them in there herself, you can infer that Danielle must be a girl of her word.

"I'm going in to talk to Mom and Dad," Dave says, putting down the knife and going into the house.

You never really work out what happened in the bucket, but you know that something did. Despite the appearance of the little fishes, Uncle Darryl and Aunt Debbie do not agree to the addition of a fishpond in the yard. So the little fishes are returned to the waters of Lake Victoria, and the bigger one is killed and eaten for dinner. And fresh Lake Victoria fish really is the best you've ever had.

THE END

"Behold!" Dave announces once you reach the top of the cliff, spreading his arms out toward the island. "The world is at our feet!"

"Don't be silly, Dave!" Danielle steps forward. "So which long way back to the boat are we going to take?"

"How about we aim for that tree over there and then come back?"

You see where he's pointing. There is a large smooth-barked spreading tree with no leaves on it sticking out of the brush near the island's left shore. "Who knows, Danny? Maybe you'll be able to climb it."

"Then what are we waiting for?" Danielle runs off happily down the hill. Dave grins and follows.

Getting to the tree does not prove to be an easy task. Sometimes you lose sight of it altogether. When you finally reach it, you find it to be growing by the lakeshore between two boulders. Danielle immediately begins to climb it. You and Dave join her.

"You guys!" Danielle calls from a branch higher up in the tree, "you need to come see this!" She's looking straight down at the water. "Just don't come out on my branch with me; it won't hold all of us."

Dave peers toward the water and then begins climbing down the tree excitedly. When looking down at the water, the first thing you notice is what looks like a whale's ribcage under the water. Looking more closely at it, you know that it must be the skeleton of a canoe, sunk just out from shore. It has probably been down there a long time. Dave is sitting comfortably on a higher branch. "You can always see things better underwater from higher positions," he comments. "Like when we flew over the lake coming here, we could see the depth of the water, submerged rocks, sandbars and all that kind of thing."

"From little mission planes, anyway," Danielle specifies. "A big plane would fly too high to see anything."

"Being a missionary pilot would be fun," Dave muses.

"Are you kidding?" Danielle says. "I would enjoy the flying part, but I couldn't handle all the loading and unloading. And the pre-flight checks...."

"They are necessary to maintain the safety of the aircraft. You know that, Danielle."

"I know, and I appreciate it very much when pilots check their planes. I just can't imagine myself flying as a career or a mission career."

Dave is staring dreamily up at the clouds.

After looking at the boat more, or as much as you can see, you determine that you probably would not have been able to see it if Lake Victoria were at its normal level. The dark shadow line on all of the white waterside boulders marks the normal water level of the lake. You doubt that anyone died when that canoe sank. Its owners probably just left it anchored in the tiny bay and returned to find it underwater.

You are glad that your aluminum canoe is chained to a tree on shore. You return to it to find a few inquisitive six-inch lizards trapped inside. You dump them out of the boat and then paddle home at five o'clock in the beginning light of the setting sun.

THE END

GLOSSARY

acha: put it down/let go (rude form)

Bao: an African game played with pebbles

baba: father

bangi (*ban-ghee*): hashish

Bei gani: How much?

chapati: soft, tortilla-like unleavened bread made with flour and oil

Chiro: night (Kizinza word **omuchiro**); also the name of the missionaries' cat

kenge (*kain-gay*): a monitor lizard

Kiswahili: the national language of Tanzania

Kizinza (*key-zin-zah*): the language of the Wazinza people

kuni (*coo-knee*): firewood

lifti (*leaf-tea*): a lift

marahaba: do it a few times

mchicha: spinach greens

Mwangika: a village two villages away from Kahunda

Mzinza: a member of the tribal group Wazinza

ndogo (*n-doe-go*): small

ndiyo (*n-dee-yo*): yes

panga (*pawn-gah*): a large multi-purpose knife; is used to cut anything from meat to firewood

sana: very

Sengerema: the nearest town with medical facilities

shikamo: the local greeting from a younger to any older person; "I grab your feet."

Simba: lion; also the name of the missionaries' dog

soko: an African marketplace

Wasukuma: the largest tribal group in Tanzania (approximately 2.5 million); Kahunda is a Wasukuma village

Wazinza: the tribal group that speaks the language Kizinza

Wazungu: Western people or white people

WHAT'S WYCLIFFE

The family you read about in this book may not be real, but they represent thousands of people who are a part of the Wycliffe team. What's Wycliffe? It's an organization of people from all over the world. What do they have in common? They all love God and value the Bible as God's Word. *And* they want everyone, everywhere, to know about God's love and be able to hear God's Word in their own language.

More than 6,800 languages are spoken in the world. About 3,000 language groups still don't have the Bible in their language. That means hundreds of millions of people have no way to hear God speak their language! How can they learn about Him? How can they have churches that teach the Word of God?

A young man named Cameron Townsend asked those questions more than 70 years ago. He was trying to give Spanish Bibles to people in Central America and realized that many of the people didn't even understand Spanish. All those languages without a Bible! Townsend was determined to do something about it. Through prayer and partnership, he started a school (SIL) and a mission organization (Wycliffe) to train people to do Bible translation and help get God's Word to the whole world.

Today about 5,000 people from all over the world are part of Wycliffe. Thousands of other people are involved, working in partnership so everyone can have God's Word in the language they understand best. A few years ago a lot of these partners met together and agreed to pursue Vision 2025. The goal of the Vision is to see Bible translation in progress for every language group that needs it by 2025.

It's a vision for all of God's people, young and old! People all over the world are praying and working together. Some people pray and give money to help fund Bible translation. Some help on short-term projects; others commit their whole lifetime. Whole churches are getting involved: youth groups, women's groups, retired people. There is something for everyone to do! Translators are needed, but you don't have to be a translator to help with Bible translation. There are teachers, computer specialists, graphic designers, office managers....

What's Wycliffe? It's people like you who want everyone to hear God's Word in the language they understand best! Learn more about how you can be involved by going to *www.wycliffe.org*.

ABOUT THE AUTHOR AND ILLUSTRATOR

Tania Matthews started writing the *East African Adventures* when she was 13 years old. She grew up as a Wycliffe missionary kid in Tanzania, Africa, where her parents served as Bible translators. Storytelling and writing have always been her hobbies. At 7 years old she began dictating stories to her mother to write down. Later she created little illustrated books using cereal boxes for covers. Tania finished high school in Kenya and currently attends the University of Tennessee at Chattanooga.

Judy Rheberg is a retired art teacher living in northeastern Wisconsin with her husband Jim. They spend winters volunteering for Wycliffe Bible Translators in Orlando, Florida. Judy loves animals. She raised sheep to save money for college and once had 10 collie dogs and 20 barn cats as pets. But Judy's all-time favorite animal is the horse. Even after plenty of rough rides and getting bucked off a time or two, she continues to love grooming, riding, reading about and drawing horses of all kinds.

Rabid dogs.
Spitting cobras.
Poisonous fish.

An afternoon in the untamed African bush offers more than a vacation – it's an adrenaline-pumping, eye-popping, life-threatening adventure. Anything is possible. You choose what happens next in this escapade that places you in the very heart of a wild African experience. Order a copy of *The Hunting Safari* today and let the adventures begin!

To order, contact Wycliffe's Media Resource Center, 1-800-992-5433, media_resource_center @wycliffe.org.

The Village Safari coming soon!